Had to Be You

an Oyster Bay novel

Olivia Miles

~ Rosewood Press ~

This is a work of fiction. Names, characters, businesses, places, events and incidents are either the products of the author's imagination or used in a fictitious manner. Any resemblance to actual persons, living or dead, or actual events is purely coincidental.

ISBN 978-0- 9995284-8-8

HAD TO BE YOU

First Edition: July 2019

Had to Be You

an Oyster Bay novel

Prologue

Chloe Larson stood at the edge of the large stone terrace with the view of the sea, nearly hidden by the flowers that anchored every corner, watching from a distance as the bride and groom stepped hand in hand onto the dance floor. As planned, every guest held a sparkler in the air, surrounding the happy couple with a glow of flickering light as they swayed to the music and gazed into each other's eyes.

Some guests teared up. Others smiled wistfully. The photographer snapped his camera.

Chloe mentally checked a box.

The cake had been cut. Plates had been cleared. The first dance was underway. There was that one little glitch where the Coast Guard decided to fly over the ceremony just before the first kiss was announced, but it only added to the anticipation, and such were the risks with outdoor weddings!

Next on her list was the bouquet toss. And where was it, exactly? Chloe glanced at the bride, just to make sure that Hannah wasn't still clutching it while she danced, but both of her hands were tightly on Dan, as they should be. Right. A bouquet to find then, and before this song ended. Chloe stepped off the terrace and walked toward the head table briskly. The sun had set over an hour ago, and the lanterns and overhead string lights that had been set up on the back lawn of the seaside estate known as Crestview Manor cast shadows on the few lingering guests who had chosen to sit out the first dance, mostly the geriatric crowd, who liked to remain seated once seated. Still, Chloe thought she noticed a younger man in their midst.

She squinted through the dark, in case it was someone she knew, but when she looked over at the table again, the man was gone. Well, no need to trouble herself with that. He was probably just keeping Mimi Harper company, especially since her husband Earl had nodded off before the dessert course. The song was winding down and Chloe's heart was speeding up. She needed to find Hannah's bouquet and bring it back to the terrace for her before the guests had one too many glasses of champagne and got carried away on the dance floor. It was always best, she had learned, for there to be an order to these things. First dance followed soon thereafter by the bouquet toss. Then everyone was free for the evening, herself included.

Chloe's shoulders sagged in relief when she spotted the colorful mixed bouquet at the head table, next to Hannah's uneaten slice of cake. It was her experience that brides rarely ate at their own wedding. They were too busy greeting guests. Too worried about spilling something on their beautiful gowns.

Hannah—with Chloe's help—had chosen cheerful summer blooms tied with a blue ribbon. Despite its weight, Chloe held it gingerly, even though it would soon be tossed into the air, where all the lonely hearts in town would scramble over each other to be the one to catch it in the hopes that this would automatically make them the next bride to grace the aisle. It was a silly tradition, but one most brides upheld, and Chloe was looking forward to it because it meant that every last item (aside from overseeing clean-up) would be scratched from her list of duties and then she could go home, ease her shoes from her aching feet, slip into her favorite cotton pajama pants, and enjoy a single glass of wine while she caught up on her favorite dating show, which she was now a week behind on, thanks to the craziness of wedding week. Not exactly what most people would consider a thrilling Saturday night, sure, but it suited her just fine.

Hannah met Chloe at the edge of the terrace to collect the bouquet, and even in the dusk, Chloe could see that her friend's cheeks were flushed and her eyes were bright. It was the happiest day of Hannah's life, Chloe thought.

Mission accomplished.

"If I were you, I probably wouldn't wait too much longer to toss this. Once the dinner is over and the cake has been cut, the party can sometimes take on a life of its own," she warned.

"I'll do it after this song," Hannah said. She looked down at the flowers and touched them softly.

It really was a shame to part with them, Chloe thought, but she nodded just the same. "I'll let the band know."

She strode across the stone terrace, teetering only slightly in her heels, and waited until the song had ended before holding up a hand.

"The bride will be tossing her bouquet now," she said to the lead singer, who appeared all too happy for a five-minute break. Chloe pursed her lips, watching the group carefully in case they decided to slip away for too long, or worse, saddle up to the bar.

Hannah moved to the center of the terrace, and all at once, like a flock of birds, every single woman in Oyster Bay over the age of eighteen was gathered at the base of the lawn. Chloe even noticed Sarah Preston's grandmother out there, bless her, and she had to be past eighty.

"Aren't you going to join them?" a voice said. It took Chloe a moment to register that the question was being directed at her.

"Excuse me?" She looked over to see the man she had seen sitting at the tables a few minutes ago. She shook her head. "No." A firm no.

"Taken then," he said, giving a shrug that matched his boyish grin.

She eyed him. Nut-brown hair. Blue-green eyes. Strong Roman nose and a nice, square jaw. Handsome. And not someone she had ever seen before in Oyster Bay.

A crasher? It was entirely possibly, but not likely. Crestview Manor was remote, at the far edge of town.

"Just sitting it out." She eyed him up and down. "Just as you chose to sit out the first dance."

His eyes flickered. "So you caught me, then."

"I notice these sorts of things," she said with a little smile.

"Between the two of us, my feet are killing me," he leaned in to say. He wiggled a foot. "New shoes."

She laughed, heard the whoop of delight rise up in the crowd as the bouquet was inevitably released, and then, fell straight backwards as it slammed into the side of her head.

She was going down. In the middle of her own event. When she wasn't even off duty. When she still had to make sure that the top tier of the cake was boxed and preserved and that the centerpieces were handed out to those who deserved them—not just to some of the greedier dates of guests who came to the weddings for the food and free drinks and sometimes didn't even know the happy couple personally.

She was going to fall. On her face? On her back. She was going to commit the cardinal sin and pull attention away from the bride.

Until someone stopped her.

She looked up into the now rather alarmed eyes of the man she had just been talking with, swallowing back her mortification as he gently righted her. Her heels wobbled underneath her and she stumbled a few steps to the side, feeling his hand tight on her elbow.

"Are you okay?" His voice filled with concern deeper than the crease between his eyebrows.

Chloe touched her head gingerly, just to make sure that there wasn't any blood, but she supposed that almost wasn't possible, considering nearly all of it had rushed to her cheeks. They burned hot with embarrassment and she nodded over and over.

"Fine. I'm fine."

He looked relieved. Even managed a smile. "That was some hit. Good thing it was just flowers."

She slanted him a glance. More like eight pounds of flowers.

"Are you okay?" Hannah came scrambling over to her, the skirt of her wedding gown hitched up in both fists, and Chloe was quick to shake her head and then nod.

"I'm fine!" She forced a smile, desperate to take herself out of the spotlight, and all at once every single woman who had been standing politely a half a dozen feet to her left made a mad sprint for the bouquet that was in a heap on the ground at her feet.

"Pick it up. Quick," the man said, and because she had just been slapped in the head by a rather large floral arrangement and because she hated to see those beautiful flowers get dirty or trampled, she did.

The groans from the crowd of women who were surging upon her were quickly drowned out by the horrible realization of what she had just done.

"You caught the bouquet!" Hannah's eyes danced with excitement as she ran back to join her new husband on the dance floor. "Chloe caught the bouquet!"

Chloe looked up at the now smirking man through the hood of her lashes. "Thanks."

"Ah, so you were hoping to catch that bouquet after all," he said.

"No, I wasn't…" But it didn't matter. Her heart was pounding and she wasn't so sure that it had anything to do with nearly falling on her face in the middle of Hannah's wedding. He had a nice smile. One of the nicest she had seen in some time. And warm, kind eyes that crinkled at the corners.

What was she thinking? She wasn't thinking at all. She had been hit in the head. She wasn't herself. Chloe Larson did eye the guests at weddings she planned. Chloe Larson didn't even date, not seriously at least. Chloe worked. And right now, she needed to get back to her job.

"Thank you," she said again. "For not letting me fall. The stone would have done a lot more damage than a fistful of botanicals."

He pointed to the flowers in her hand. They had weathered the fall better than she had. She'd be sure to praise her friend Posy for her excellent floral arranging.

"That's not just any bouquet. It means you're next to be married, right?" He shoved his hands into the pockets of his pants, giving her a long, knowing look. Chloe watched him, taking in his face, wondering how he'd acquired that scar on his chin that was his only physical flaw and made him all the more attractive, and then cleared her throat.

Really! She was on the clock.

"If you believe in superstition, I suppose," Chloe said.

"You mean, you don't?" His eyes gleamed.

"I believe in tradition," she said firmly.

"Then that means you'll be holding onto it," he said, motioning to the bouquet.

She sighed deeply, looking down at the bouquet. She really didn't need the hassle of carrying it around when she needed to check on that cake tier.

She smoothed the skirt of her shift dress, wondered if she had a mark on her cheek from where she'd been hit, and then touched the side of her head, alarmed that some of her hair had been pulled from its chignon.

"I should…go tend to this," she said, feeling a strange urge to stay right where she was, even though duty called and this man was a guest, and one which she technically should be tending to, not the other way around. "Thank you. Again."

"The honor was all mine," he said, and slowly, almost reluctantly, she thought, he walked away, pausing only to give her one last grin over his shoulder.

Chapter One

Chloe checked the time on her watch as she slowed to a walk. Three minutes faster than yesterday. Not bad. Not great either, especially if she wanted to finish in the top ten at this fall's Turkey Trot. Still, there was always another chance after work today, and she could blame the anticipation of this morning's big meeting for being distracted.

Quickly, she pushed through the door of her apartment building, sprinted up the two flights of stairs, wincing when she heard the pounding on the wall from Amanda Quinn in the unit below, reminding her that not everyone was ready to start their day, something Chloe still couldn't wrap her head around. What good was sleep when there was a day to be filled, work to be done, goals to be met? When she woke every morning, her mind was already bursting with her task list, an entire mental inventory of what needed to be accomplished before she climbed under the covers again. She couldn't imagine languishing in bed, delaying her start. That was how people fell behind.

Besides, her anxiety trumped any pleasure she derived from the warm comfort of her down duvet.

By seven thirty, she was showered and dressed in a lake blue linen sheath, which she'd set out the night before, along with all the necessary accessories (shoes, necklace, earrings, handbag), and her blonde hair was pulled back in a chignon, her preferred look. She'd already clocked a five-mile run. Already eaten her usual breakfast: one poached egg with a slice of gluten-free toast and a cup of coffee. Her teeth were brushed. Her bed was made (with hotel corners because the extra effort paid off at the end of the day as extra efforts usually did). Her gym clothes were already tumbling in her in-unit washing machine, one she had installed herself in her hall closet when Trudy, a lonely widow across the hall who made everything about the building her personal business, accused her of using up the basement facility too much. Was it Chloe's fault that she had a system? Sheets each Sunday. Towels each Saturday. Clothes…well, usually daily.

"Doesn't a pretty girl like you have anything better to do than worry about laundry?" Trudy had shaken her head, clucking her tongue in disappointment, but Chloe wasn't stung. Well, not really. She liked things in order. It brought her happiness. Was that really so unusual for a woman of her age?

Apparently, it was. After all, most of her friends were in relationships now. Some were married. More would be engaged soon by the look of things. And Chloe hadn't had a date since…well, no need to dwell on that.

Chloe locked the door to her apartment and ran down the stairs, until the banging started again and then she had to slow herself to a suppressed skip. A surge of excitement swelled in her chest as her heeled feet hit the pavement outside her building. Her apartment was one block off Main Street, something she had chosen specifically more than seven years ago when she first opened her shop.

She walked briskly to the corner and then turned onto Oyster Bay's main strip, which was still quiet at this hour. Angie's Café would be open, of course. Maybe Jojo's. Trish would be just getting in over at Books by the Bay. Chip down at The Lantern would have already clocked three hours, if not four, making sure he had the finest catch to offer his customers come the lunch hour.

And then there were the new shops, new restaurants, more each day, it seemed. At first this had unsettled her. Change was full of uncertainty, wasn't it? But so far the Main Street revitalization project had boosted the local economy, bringing in more tourists, and keeping them there. Her friend Bridget who owned the Harper House

Inn had remarked that they were booked up through Labor Day.

Bayside Brides was just ahead now. Quiet and sleepy, waiting for someone to come and wake it up. The awning that usually flapped in the ocean breeze was still today. It was a hot, sticky day, even for early August. The month would bring a surge of late-summer people, and then September would slow, with kids back in school. Business would wind down. It always did come fall.

But Chloe couldn't worry about that today. Today Chloe had a meeting with Lori Addison, editor of *Here Comes the Bride* magazine, who was planning a spring wedding right here in Oyster Bay. It was a pinch-me moment, and Chloe still didn't feel like it was actually happening, even though she'd triple-checked Lori's confirmation email last night. She could not let anything ruin this opportunity.

She hurried to unlock the door to the store and get settled. By the time she had freshened up the bouquets, spruced up the front planters, straightened the back office space, and made sure even the glass of the windows shone, Melanie Dillon, her co-owner and cousin, had finally arrived to work.

Chloe knew that both Melanie and their assistant Sarah Preston thought she expected too much from them. And they were never late, that was true. But they just didn't have the same passion as she did. They also, she realized, didn't share the same anxiety. After all, wasn't that what brought her into work early each day and kept her here late each day?

Well, that and the fact that she had nothing else to do with her time, really. Other than run or hit the gym. Melanie was in a relationship. And recently, Sarah had also found romance.

"Ready for the big meeting?" Melanie asked with large eyes as she swung her handbag on a hook in the back room.

Chloe said nothing as she took it and moved it into a cabinet. Normally, she would have let this slide, but then, she had never had a meeting with Lori Addison before.

"If she even shows up," Chloe said. It felt like a relief to reveal her biggest fear out loud. The very one that had kept her up for three hours in the middle of the night, until she had to chant, "sleep, sleep, sleep" to herself until it finally came, two hours before her alarm went off. She could have skipped the morning jog, perhaps, but she knew what happened when you started letting things slip: nothing good.

"Of course she'll be here!" Melanie looked at her like she was crazy and gave her a good-natured pat on the arm as she walked back into the storefront. "Didn't she confirm just yesterday?"

Chloe nodded. She had, of course she had. Lori would be spending the weekend in Oyster Bay. Her Friday morning meeting with Chloe was her first stop.

"And there she is!" Melanie all but cried just as Chloe felt all the blood rush from her face.

She should have had some fruit this morning. Something for her blood pressure. She was a bag of nerves, but who wouldn't be? Lori Addison. Editor of Chloe's absolute favorite wedding magazine. Here, in her shop.

Melanie didn't know what Lori looked like anymore than Chloe did, of course, but the woman approaching the store was unmistakably Lori. She was all city, for one. Black, head to toe. Most people in Oyster Bay preferred something a little lighter in color this time of year: seersucker, linen, whites and blues and corals.

Her sole splash of color was in her handbag. Bright pink. Huge. And speaking of huge—her sunglasses covered nearly half her face, giving her an air of celebrity flair. She looked every bit the part of big city editor and not blushing bride to be as they had come to expect here at Bayside Brides. And yet…here she was. To see if Chloe had what it took to plan her wedding.

She removed her sunglasses as she entered the shop, her shoulder-length brown hair swishing as she glanced from Chloe to Melanie and back again. "Chloe Larson?" She extended a hand. Her smile was disarmingly warm.

"Lori," Chloe said, her eyes widening only a notch at the crushing grip. "It's so nice to meet you. Hannah's told me so much about you."

Not exactly true, considering that Hannah and Dan were currently on their honeymoon, but Hannah was the connecting piece. The two women had worked together for a while at a fashion magazine in California, and after seeing pictures of Hannah's wedding, Lori had made a call.

Chloe had already planned her thank-you gift to Hannah. High tea at the Oyster Bay Hotel, a special and rare treat.

"Please, come back to the office. We can discuss everything."

On shaking legs, she walked past Melanie, who gave her an almost imperceptible wink and then crossed to answer the phone with a crisp, "Bayside Brides?"

Good, good. Even at this early hour, they looked busy.

The back office room was all ready for this meeting. Her vision board was propped on an easel. The water had been chilled and flavored with fresh berries which had sunk to the bottom. The music was light and calming. The flowers on the center of the table, purchased yesterday at Morning Glory down the street, were colorful and modern in their arrangement.

She was ready!

"Water?" Her voice was tight as she brought the pitcher and two glasses to the table. She poured as Lori settled into a chair and admired the fabric samples spread out before her for bridesmaid dresses. (Lori had been clear in her first email that her gown was being purchased in Manhattan.)

"It's funny," Lori said. "I *never* thought I would be having a wedding in a small town like this," she seemed to laugh and look at Chloe as if she, too, should agree that this really was ridiculous. But Chloe just smiled, because she loved Oyster Bay, loved her small, coastal community with the white picket fences and overflowing hydrangea bushes, the cedar shingled homes that lined the coast, and the lull of the ocean.

She almost questioned Lori on her decision to hold her wedding here, but Lori had been clear to stress in her email that her wedding was going to be the cover story for *Here Comes the Bride*'s "country weddings" issue.

Chloe had to press her lips together to suppress her excitement every time she thought of it.

"Oyster Bay is a lovely town," Chloe said encouragingly. "It's classic New England. It's...authentic. Sure, we have our share of tourists, but what we pride ourselves on is that so many generations have grown up here through the ages. I'm a local myself."

Lori raised an eyebrow. "You never left?"

"Oh, for design school," Chloe was quick to explain. "But I knew when I started my business that this was where I wanted to be. We started as a boutique, but as we've grown, we never lost sight of our philosophy. I believe that every wedding should be personal, purposeful, and perfect."

"Personal, purposeful, and perfect," Lori said wistfully. "I love that. I may have to quote you."

Chloe hoped her smile wasn't too eager. She took a sip of water to steady herself. "Now, based on our conversation, I put together a few ideas for you to consider, but of course I thought we could discuss your vision in more detail."

Lori's eyes drifted to the vision board that Chloe had labored over for the past two days. To Chloe's relief, she seemed to like what she saw.

"Tulips won't do, though," she said, frowning. "I prefer seasonal flowers."

"Well, for spring—" Chloe started, but then Lori shook her head.

"We had a snafu," she said, rolling her eyes as she reached for her water. "Just found out about it late last night."

"A snafu?" Chloe could already feel her stomach twisting into knots, the same way it always did growing up, when she was looking particularly forward to something and her father walked in the door an hour earlier than he was expected, and she heard her mother's voice, low and concerned through the kitchen wall, and she didn't need to wait to be told that there would be no birthday party this year, or back to school shopping spree this year, or whatever it was that Chloe had pinned such hope to.

Of course there was a snafu. There was always a snafu. Why had she dared to think that this time it might be different?

"Our October issue had to be reworked," Lori started to explain, even though Chloe didn't quite understand what October had to do with her planned May wedding. "It was supposed to be a destination theme, but, well, long story short the entire bridal party got food poisoning. Rehearsal dinner. Undercooked fish. It happens." She shrugged.

Did it happen? In her endless lists of everything that could go wrong, Chloe had somehow failed to consider this one. Now…well, now it was all she could think about. She would lose sleep thinking about this, she was sure. She considered her upcoming weddings. She would review their menus, directly after this. She'd call the caterers, too. Just to have a little chitchat about expectations.

"So, we've decided to move that edition to the spring and bring the country issue up to October. It's a scramble, but we're able to pull some stories that were supposed to go in November and December, and they promised they could drop the cover story right in at the final hour."

Chloe gaped at her. "Meaning…"

"Meaning it looks like I'm getting married at the end of the month!"

"End of…*this* month?" Chloe swallowed hard, and she had the horrible sensation that she was gaping. In their brief conversation on Monday, Lori had mentioned something in the vicinity of two hundred guests, maybe two-fifty. And the Harper House Inn was booked up. The Oyster Bay Hotel likely was too.

And why was she even worried about where all the out-of-town guests would stay? Where would they even hold the wedding on such short notice?

"This is short notice." She stared at her hands on the table, her mind spinning, and she wondered if Lori could see the panic in her face. Four weeks. She was talking four weeks! "Have you considered a specific location you'd like to use?"

"Don't worry," Lori said, holding up a hand. "The guests have all been notified by email. Invitations will be a formality, still a necessary one, though. And I already have things locked in at the Oyster Bay Hotel. We have access to their terrace and private beachfront. It's all part of the perks," she said with a little smile.

Yes, Chloe supposed it would be, considering the clout that the magazine held. She felt her shoulders sink in relief. "Well, good."

It would be tight. Too tight for her comfort. But what other choice was there? She'd make it happen. The chance for Bayside Brides to get this much exposure was just too good to pass up.

Besides, when did she ever shy away from hard work?

"I have a good feeling about you, Chloe," Lori said, giving her a hundred-watt smile.

Chloe waited on bated breath to see what Lori would say next. Did she have the job? Or would she go with the in-house event planner at the Oyster Bay Hotel? Neil was a scatterbrain, if anyone were to ask her, but she'd crossed paths with him enough times to coexist in a professional capacity, even if she did have to suppress a sigh every time he air-kissed her on each cheek and then insisted on calling her (and every other female he encountered) "darling."

"I'll admit that I did have my doubts. And I have my event planner back in New York on notice, who would be all too happy to get out of the city for a few weeks. But…" She drummed her fingers on the table, twisting her lips as she scrutinized the vision board. It would all have to be scrapped now. The flowers. Maybe even the color scheme. But it was exquisite. Possibly Chloe's finest work yet. And she had a feeling that Lori saw that, too.

"I know everyone in town," Chloe said, careful not to come across too eager. "Catering, flowers. I'm on very good terms with the *coordinator* at the Oyster Bay Hotel," she said carefully.

"And of course the wedding you planned for Hannah was divine," Lori said. "Or at least the photographs were. It was a shame I had to miss it, but work comes first!"

"I couldn't agree more," Chloe said, sparking a curious glance from Lori.

"Are you married?"

Chloe gave a serene smile. "Only to my job."

Lori laughed, but Chloe could tell she wasn't ready to drop the subject just yet.

"Anyone special in your life?"

Chloe paused, thinking of the man she had met at Hannah's wedding, but quickly pushed the absurd thought away. He was a wedding guest. Certainly not from town.

"No one special," she said. At least, not yet. Someday. When the timing was right.

"Well, I have a feeling that *my* someone special is going to like you a lot," Lori said as she pushed back her chair.

Chloe stood, her heart thumping against her ribcage, wondering if this was it, or if Lori would leave her dangling. Or stick with her contact back in the city.

"He's got some business here in town," Lori was saying. She looped her handbag straps over her forearm.

"And what does he do?" Chloe asked, eager to continue the conversation. She couldn't let Lori go, not yet, not without an answer.

"Oh, real estate. Commercial stuff." Lori wiggled a hand in the air as if she couldn't make sense of it.

"Well, there's certainly a lot of expansion happening in town at the moment. You couldn't have picked a better time to hold your wedding."

"And I have a feeling I couldn't have picked a better wedding planner either," Lori said, giving her a big grin.

Chloe felt her eyes widen as the air slumped out of her. Good grief, she'd done it. She'd actually done it. Her hand felt weak as she extended it to Lori, and soon they were talking all at once, excitedly, about flowers and color schemes and the next meeting.

"Is tomorrow morning good for you?"

"Perfect," Chloe said as she escorted Lori to the front door of the shop. She was more than a little aware of Melanie's and Sarah's eyes on her while they tried their best to look busier than they were.

She waited until Lori was out of view before turning around, facing the other two women, and exclaiming, "We got it!"

The wedding of all weddings. The cover of a nationally distributed magazine. So it was in a month. She could pull it together.

It would be the most beautiful wedding ever to be seen in Oyster Bay.

Nothing could ruin it. And she had a feeling, in her sudden burst of optimism, that nothing would.

Chapter Two

This morning Chloe was going to do it. She could feel it. A seven-minute mile, five miles in a row.

Whereas most people in town preferred to jog along the shore, Chloe found that the park was best, specifically the trail around the duck pond. At this early hour, few people were out and about, and she didn't have to worry about dodging a biker or a kid tossing crumbs at the birds.

She was just coming in for the final lap. A quarter of a mile to go. She resisted the urge to glance at her watch—it would only slow her down. Her legs felt it. Her chest felt it. She was at maximum capacity. She was on fire. And it was all because of yesterday's big boost, of that she was sure.

A wedding on the cover of *Here Comes the Bride* magazine. Something she had only dreamed of, and not in the realistic sense. Something that hadn't seemed possible, but now it was actually happening. All that work had paid off.

She pushed forward a little harder, careful not to push too hard and lose her footing. She was almost there. So close. It was all within reach.

Her eyes caught someone up ahead as she rounded the bend; someone who was noticeably slower than she, a man, tall, lean but with an athletic build.

"On your right!" she called out as she approached.

The man did nothing. Didn't flinch. Didn't turn around. Damn headphones. It was why she never wore them when she ran. She didn't want to be that oblivious to her surroundings. Didn't want to ever lose sight of what was coming, or be taken by surprise.

Preparation was always best. In all areas of life.

"On your right!" she managed, but she was out of breath, the force of shouting was slowing her down, and she gritted her teeth, hoping that her toe didn't catch the man's heel as she edged past him, up onto the slope of grass that hugged the paved path, knowing that had cost her a few seconds at least.

She didn't stop until she had reached the old bench where the path forked and the road led back to town. She looked at her watch, grinning through the sweat that was blurring her vision. Good. But it could have been better if she hadn't been forced to veer off course.

"That was quite a pace you had," the man said, and she looked up, startled to see that it was the same man from the wedding.

She remembered the sweat that was beaded at her brow, tickling its way down the slope of her cheek near her ear. Hardly her best look. She was panting, her hands on her hips, waiting for her heart rate to slow, but now, she didn't see any chance of it.

"I was wondering if I'd run into you again," he said, and then, after a beat: "No pun intended."

She laughed, harder than the joke warranted, really, but she needed to release it. The nerves, the excitement. So the mystery man was still in town. And that...well, that was certainly interesting.

"I'm Nick, by the way," he said and extended a hand.

She reached out and took it, hoping that her palm wasn't too sweaty. But his hand felt warm in hers, smooth and firm. And...nice.

"I'm Chloe," she said.

"Chloe," he repeated, softly, narrowing his gaze slightly on the word, as if he were pondering it carefully. He fell into step beside her, and she decided that, given her time, she could spare an extra cool-down lap around the pond before heading back to her apartment to get ready for work.

"I haven't seen you here before," she said. "I...haven't seen you in Oyster Bay before." It was a small community, after all. Other than tourists, most people knew each other, at least casually.

"I'm new. Well, temporarily," he said. "I'm in town for a while on business." He glanced at her. "You're an early riser."

"Don't see any sense in sleeping away the day," she said with a shrug. Usually this type of comment sparked an eye roll from her cousin Melanie or a look of dismay from her mother, but Nick just grinned.

"So this is your regular path, then?"

She didn't know where he was going with this. Maybe he was just being conversational. Maybe he was wondering if she was territorial (she hoped she hadn't given that away). Or maybe…She swallowed hard and darted her eyes up at him. Damn, he was cute. His nut-brown hair was scruffy this morning and his eyes…in the crisp morning light they were decidedly more green than blue, something she hadn't noticed at the wedding last Saturday.

"It is," she said. "I'm sort of a creature of habit, that way."

"I hope you don't mind me breaking up your routine then," he said, giving her a questioning look that almost passed for flirtatious when she caught the curl of his mouth.

Normally, the mere idea of having her routine interrupted was distressing, but to her surprise she realized she was all too happy to rearrange things a bit. Besides, she had finished her run, and in good time too.

"Well, I do owe you, after all," she said, grinning. Their legs were moving in stride, she realized. Right, left, right, left. "It's not every day I get hit in the head with a bouquet of flowers."

"Well, you at least got something out of it," he said. "Flowers. A husband?"

She laughed. "Half the time it's a teenage girl catching the bouquet. Once, I saw a seventy-four-year-old widow catch it. Well, she didn't actually catch it. It fell into her lap. Still. It's what brides like to do."

"And you think it's silly."

She gave him a rueful look. "Like I told you, I think it's…tradition."

"Well, so is the chicken dance," he pointed out, and at this she laughed again.

"You seem to know an awful lot about weddings," she mused, thinking that most of the men she knew didn't pay as much attention to these types of things.

But Nick just shrugged. "I've attended my share."

Attended. Confirming he'd never been married.

She let that thought sink in for a moment. Dared to smile a bit about it.

They were rounding the end of the lap, and she realized that their time was quickly fading. She bit back the disappointment, chastised herself for even thinking of being late for work, especially when she had another meeting with Lori Addison this morning.

"Well," she said. "I suppose I should get home to shower. I have an appointment this morning."

"Me too," he said, and it was only then that she realized she had actually been the one to interrupt his routine, not the other way around.

"But you didn't get your run in!" she apologized.

He just grinned down at her. "This was better."

She licked her lips to hide her smile as they turned onto the road that led back into town. The walk was short; the park was just at the end of Main Street, and she slowed her pace, wanting to delay her arrival at her apartment.

"So Nick, what keeps you here in Oyster Bay?"

"It's not completely official, but I'm in talks to buy the Oyster Bay Hotel," he said in a low voice that made her feel like she was a coconspirator. A willing one.

Her eyes shot open in surprise. "Impressive!" She blinked a few times, trying to understand what this could mean. Lori Addison wanted her wedding there. And soon. And nothing could stand in the way of that wedding being anything but perfect. "Will anything change?" she dared to ask, holding her breath.

"Only for the better, I hope." He smiled and rolled back on his heels. "We're still in talks, but if all goes as planned, we should have the deal wrapped up by the end of the month. And then the real work begins."

"We?" She glanced at his hand just to be sure she hadn't missed anything. No ring.

"My father's company," he explained. "Family business."

"What kind of work do you have planned, if you don't mind me asking?" She was partial to that hotel. She personally liked it just the way it was, and so did plenty of other people in town, she knew. Sure, it was a little dated, but it wasn't by any measure rundown. It was nostalgic; it spoke to another time, a simpler time, perhaps, at least for her.

"I don't mind at all," Nick said. "We're still in the planning stages, but most of the work would be structural improvements. Window replacements, upgrading elevators, and renovating some of the suites."

"So nothing too major then," Chloe said, not bothering to hide her relief. It would be a shame if the wallpaper was stripped and the charm ripped out, after all. "All those beautiful French doors will stay in place?"

"Oh, absolutely!" Nick was quick to say. "And the feel won't change either. But some of the carpet is worn out, and the upholstery too. It's my belief that a property can be renovated without losing its essence."

She smiled. "If you need a contractor—" But then she stopped. Of course. Dan was a contractor, and the best in town. He'd taken over his father's business, learned the job from a young age. "I understand now. You know Dan. That's why you were at the wedding."

"Dan's a great guy. We've been talking about this project for a few weeks now, but I'm guessing he never mentioned anything because we weren't sure it would go through."

"And will it?" Chloe asked. She decided then and there that she hoped it would. Badly.

"It should." Nick grinned, and Chloe met his eye for a moment longer than she usually did when talking to people, and smiled.

Chloe looked away, feeling secure with the standing of Lori's wedding. If ownership changed, she doubted that Nick would do anything to cause trouble for her where this wedding was concerned.

"Dan's a good friend. Highly recommended," she said.

"Back from his honeymoon soon, I hope."

"Today." Not that she was keeping tabs, when, in fact, she had been planning to ask Hannah about her mystery guest upon her return from Italy, as well as glean as much information as she could about her old friend Lori Addison.

"I owe him a round of drinks," Nick said. "You should come too, bring Hannah along. Now that I might be sticking around town, it would be nice to have a few familiar faces."

Oh would it? Now her heart was positively racing and she swallowed back her excitement, clung to something safer, something easier to discuss than how much she would really love to go on a double date with him and Hannah and Dan. She might even make an exception and agree to it before the end of the month, despite all the work she'd have to do for Lori's wedding.

"And how are you finding our town so far?" she asked.

He gave her a grin that seemed to spread all the way to his eyes and said, "It's really starting to have a lot of potential." Their eyes locked long enough for Chloe to take a sharp breath as her stomach did a strange little dance.

Oh boy.

His phone beeped and he looked down, muttering under his breath as he did so. "Duty calls. But if this is your usual route, I'll probably be seeing you again soon," he said as he edged backward, toward town, his eyebrows lifted into a question. His smile was wide and open. It was, she thought, an invitation.

She grinned. "You can count on it."

*

Melanie gave her a strange look when Chloe walked into Bayside Brides, admittedly, a solid twelve minutes later than usual.

"You look nice this morning," she said.

Chloe glanced down at her outfit, a pink A-line skirt and white Swiss dot blouse specifically selected for her second meeting with Lori. After all, one could never be too careful. What if Lori had had a change of heart over night? What if the groom didn't like her?

"You look...different," Melanie continued. Her eyes seemed to narrow.

Immediately, Chloe frowned. "Different? Different how?"

"Oh, not in a bad way," Melanie was quick to assure her. She hesitated. "Don't take this the wrong way, but you look, almost…happy."

"As if that's such a rare occurrence," Chloe remarked as she walked to the back room to get set up for the meeting. But it was a rare occurrence, and she was happy. Happy about Bayside Brides and Lori's wedding and all the publicity they would gain from the magazine exposure. Happy about Nick, she thought, with a little smile.

"I'm just feeling…hopeful."

Melanie's eyes nearly crossed. "That's so…optimistic of you!"

Chloe shook her head, but she knew that Melanie had a point. She wasn't exactly a glass half-full type of girl, and she didn't see how she ever could be. In her experience, there had been too much probability of that glass spilling, of being left with nothing, of feeling more let down than necessary. It was always best to prepare for the worst.

"I'm fully capable of being an optimist," she said, as she walked over to inspect the bouquet of flowers in the center of the room. She slanted a glance back at her cousin. "A *guarded* optimist."

Melanie didn't look convinced. "You don't even believe the weather forecasts when rain isn't expected for weeks."

"Outdoor weddings are risky," Chloe pointed out as she walked over to check that the tiaras and veils were all neatly in place. She fluffed some tulle on the veils, then stood back. Much better.

"You track the order of every dress, even though we've never had one disappear."

"I'm just keeping tabs on things," Chloe's chin rose a notch. "You can never be too careful." She walked over to the rack of shoes. Two of the samples were askew, she noted with a frown. She straightened them to her satisfaction.

Melanie shook her head. "If I didn't know better, I'd say—" She stopped herself. Gave Chloe a critical squint. "No. Never mind."

But Chloe knew what Melanie had been about to say. That Chloe was in love.

Preposterous! Just as Melanie knew it was. Besides, how could Chloe be in love? She had only met Nick twice, on brief occasions. That wasn't love. That was just…hope.

"So, did you celebrate last night?" Melanie asked as she followed Chloe into the back room. Without being asked, she started a pot of coffee, and Chloe noticed that there were notepads and pens already set out on the table.

Chloe had considered dusting off a bottle of champagne last night, but the thought of drinking it alone seemed anything but celebratory. "I worked out," she said, and Melanie tsked.

"Does nothing make you ever switch up your routine?"

Chloe bit her lip. She was fairly certain that Melanie would be surprised to hear that she had been all too capable of changing her routine this morning, but she didn't have time to get into that. Lori would be here any minute.

"I don't want to jinx myself," she said. And it was true. Not about Lori Addison's wedding. Not about Nick. She pulled in a sigh, drawing up a mental picture of his face. Pushed away a smile. "I'll celebrate once the wedding is over."

Melanie just shook her head. "You have to learn to embrace the good things when they happen. Lori said she wanted you to plan her wedding. That's cause for celebration, not worry."

Chloe didn't bother correcting her. After all, how could she not worry? A hundred things could go wrong with any given wedding, and she was now prepared for all of them, even the possibility of food poisoning from a rehearsal dinner.

The wedding bells that hung from the front door jangled in the distance, and Chloe felt her stomach roll over. She wasn't ready. The coffee hadn't finished brewing and she had wanted to set up her laptop so the presentation of tablescape ideas she'd put together last night in lieu of the champagne was already playing when Lori arrived.

"It's Sarah," Melanie said, as if reading her mind, and she probably had. Melanie was the closest thing to a sibling Chloe had, after all, even though their childhoods were vastly different, despite both growing up in this town. Melanie's family was traditional: four-bedroom house, two kids, Sunday night dinners in the dining room, annual trips to the amusement park, zoo, and a big trip into Boston or New York City for some museums and culture.

Whereas Chloe's childhood…

"I just saw Lori coming down the block," Sarah said in a stage whisper as she poked her head around the open doorframe.

Chloe cut a glance to the coffee. It was almost finished brewing, but she hoped to get the tray set up before her clients arrived.

"Since we're rolling out the red carpet, I stopped at Angie's on my way in," Sarah said, holding out a box of croissants. "I hope that's okay?"

Chloe felt her shoulders sag in relief. "More than okay. You're a lifesaver. Thank you!" Why hadn't she thought of that herself?

Oh. Right. Because she had been thinking about Nick.

She set the croissants on a plate, doubting that Lori would even touch one, but the gesture was nice. She had just finished powering up her laptop when the bells jangled once more and she heard Melanie greet the guests who had arrived. Lori's voice was clear and crisp. The man's voice was less audible.

Chloe smoothed her skirt, tucked a loose strand of hair behind her ear, and walked toward the door to the storefront.

And locked eyes with Nick.

She faltered, her heart beginning to pound so loudly that she was sure it could heard by everyone in the room. Sarah was beaming from behind the guests, and Melanie was looking at her expectantly, her brow pinching just a notch because, well, she knew her too well.

Lori, however, seemed unfazed. "Sorry if we're late," she said, hoisting her oversized bag onto her other arm. "Nick decided to take a longer than usual jog this morning."

Was that so? Chloe blinked at Lori, unsure of what she knew, and decided from the annoyed look on Lori's face that she knew nothing. That maybe there was nothing to tell. That the man standing here before her, looking just as cornered as she felt, wasn't Lori's fiancé at all, but rather…her brother?

Putting all doubts aside, Lori said, "Chloe, this is Nicholas Tyler, my fiancé. Nick, this is Chloe Larson. Our wedding planner."

His eyes never strayed from hers, and she appraised him coolly, managing somehow a tight smile. After a beat, she extended her hand, her chest tightening slightly as he took it. His palm was warm, his grip firm, his skin just as smooth as it had been a short while ago. Her body betrayed her, as every nerve seemed to rise to attention, and she wanted to keep holding it as much as she wanted to drop it. His gaze seemed to want to tell her something. A secret message. As if they were in cahoots or something, as if this were nothing more than when he'd revealed he might be buying the Oyster Bay Hotel.

The Oyster Bay Hotel. Now it all clicked. Lori had contacts, she'd said. Well, she certainly did!

"Nice to meet you, Nick," Chloe said crisply, snatching her hand back. It tingled at her side, and she glanced at Melanie, who was really frowning at her now. She huffed out a breath and looked at Lori. "Shall we get started?"

"Absolutely," Lori said, moving toward the back room. "I've been brainstorming ideas and I brought a few back issues with me, if you don't mind. I just need this wedding to be perfect."

"It will be," Chloe said on autopilot.

Only she wasn't so sure about that anymore. In fact, once again, just like always, she wasn't sure of anything.

Chapter Three

Nick didn't meet her eyes as he took a chair across the table, beside Lori. Chloe tried to keep the tremor out of her hands as she carried the pitcher of water to the table and said, "Coffee?"

She felt a flush creep up in her cheeks and she quickly walked to the counter and grabbed the carafe of coffee, but she thought she detected a glimmer of amusement pass through Nick's gaze when he glanced her way.

Was this so funny to him? One big, happy coincidence?

Maybe it was, she thought sadly. After all, this was a man who was here to plan his wedding. This morning, much like last Saturday, clearly hadn't meant much more than a passing thought to him. Whereas to her...

Well.

"Coffee or water," she said, coming back to the table. Damn. Her voice was strained. Her nerves showed through. Or rather, her discomfort.

Nick helped himself to water and gulped it down.

Chloe clicked around on her laptop, eager to get started on her PowerPoint presentation, but she kept clicking the wrong button, and her palms were slick with sweat, making the cursor travel all over the screen instead of where she wanted it to go.

Oh, to excuse herself. To call in Sarah or Melanie and bolt out the back door.

Instead she kept her eyes trained on the screen, hoping that her clients wouldn't hear the pounding of her heart.

Engaged. The man was engaged. And here she was thinking that he was looking forward to seeing her again, that he had even alluded to a double date.

She looked at him sharply, causing him to sputter on his water.

Lori reached out and patted his back, hard, in a way that made her seem almost bored, as if the mere thought of touching him, feeling his body under her palm, was something that had grown old.

Chloe remembered the feel of his hand on her elbow, his hands on her back, and she had to look away. Focus on the screen. On the PowerPoint presentation.

That's all she could do, and she would do it, because she had worked long and hard and sacrificed way too much, including the feeling that she had dared to feel just this week, for this moment.

She reached out to fill her own water glass and brushed hands with Nick, who was reaching for the pitcher at the same time. A bolt of something warm and thrilling shot through her like fire, and she met his eye, snatching her hand back and quickly replacing it back on the keyboard. But even as she fumbled with the buttons, she could still feel the warmth of his hand, the smoothness of his skin, on her fingertips.

Finally, the presentation came up, and she forced a bright smile, kept her eyes on the screen. "Well," she said, in her most professional tone. "Let's get started."

*

Any hope that Chloe had of pretending *that* didn't just happen evaporated the moment that Lori and her fiancé—Chloe closed her eyes at the mere thought of it— disappeared out the door, after agreeing to meet up tomorrow at eleven at the Oyster Bay Hotel.

Melanie cornered her as she beelined for the back room.

"I have to clean up," Chloe protested. Really, she just needed to get away. To think. To breathe. To push this heavy weight out of her chest. Nick! It was Nick! The very man that she had dared to think about these past few days had turned out to be the groom in the biggest wedding of her career!

She wanted to call him a jerk. Wanted to be disgusted with him, really. And maybe she should be. But a part of her couldn't help but think she had just misread his friendliness for…interest.

Maybe Melanie was right. Maybe she did need to get out more, make more time for fun.

But then, look what happened when she did!

"Wasn't that the guy from Hannah's wedding?" Melanie asked as she followed her into the back room. "The one who helped you up when the bouquet hit you in the face?"

Darn. There was no sense in pretending otherwise. Half the guests had witnessed what happened, after all.

She nodded once. "It was. Small world." But then, not so small at all, she thought, as the puzzle slowly came together. Sure, Nick knew Dan, but that wasn't the reason he was at the wedding, at least, not originally. He had been invited because Lori and Hannah were friends. And Lori couldn't make it. But Nick still went because he'd become chummy with Dan.

The man may have been alone at the wedding, but he wasn't single. Far from it.

"I'm surprised you didn't say anything about it," Melanie continued. "You pretended that you didn't know him."

Chloe felt her cousin's eyes on her as she closed her laptop containing the presentation she'd made for the meeting and stored it on a file cabinet. She didn't even want to think about that wedding again, or Lori, or Nick for that matter. She'd managed to stare mostly at the screen for the entire thirty minutes, discussing flower options and centerpiece shape and bridesmaid dress styles, and everything else that she'd so carefully planned. So much for that.

She dumped the remaining coffee from the pot down the sink and ran the water, drowning out the thumping of her heart.

"Oh," she said. Her voice was tight instead of casual, as she had intended. "No sense in retelling that moment to Lori Addison, of all people. I don't want her thinking I'm unprofessional or anything."

Which was exactly what Lori would think if she got wind of Chloe's little run-in with Nick earlier this morning, or the fact that she'd closed her eyes and pulled up an image of his face while she got ready for work. For this very meeting!

"But isn't it strange that he didn't say something?" Melanie pressed. "I mean, why hide it from his fiancée?"

Chloe was happy her back was to her cousin so that Melanie wouldn't see the frown that was pulling at her eyebrows. It was a good point. And not one she had an excuse ready for, either.

After all, if their only encounter had been at the wedding, there would have been nothing to hide. But this morning…this morning had felt different. Like the start of something.

More like the end of something, she told herself. All that hope. Pouf. She should have known better.

Chloe shrugged as she dried her hands on a towel.

"Maybe he was taking my lead? Anyway, Lori is all business, so he probably just wanted to get on with the meeting."

Melanie didn't look convinced. "Maybe," she said.

Or maybe he hadn't said anything because he knew that there was something more, something wrong. That a line had been crossed. And that now there was no going back.

*

Nick stared at his open menu, barely digesting a word. Lori was talking, something about the wedding, but he wasn't paying attention. He couldn't pay attention. The girl from the wedding. Christ, the girl from this morning. Their wedding planner.

Chloe. The moment she had said her name, he thought it sounded familiar, but it was a common enough name that he let the idea drop. And what was he supposed to say at that point, anyway? Are you by any chance a wedding planner, because hey, I'm getting married.

That's actually what he should have done, he told himself. Except that he was struggling to accept it himself.

He'd seen the look in her eyes, the confusion, the uncertainty. The judgment. She probably thought he was the biggest jerk in the world. And maybe he was, chatting with a pretty girl, not revealing his relationship status. He was getting married at the end of the month. Married!

And all he could think about was that he didn't feel the way he should, that a man about to promise himself to a woman in a month's time should be nervous, sure, but excited, happy, and more at peace.

Instead he was struggling to sleep. And he was overeating. Never a good sign.

"Nick?" Lori's voice cut through his thoughts and he glanced up, noticing the impatience that was now etched in her face. "You haven't been paying attention to a word I've been saying."

He set down the menu. He'd order a burger. Keep it simple. No more big decisions.

"You know that when it comes to all this wedding planning, I defer to you," he said, and not by choice, but by convenience. Some things were just easier that way. Heck, as of a few days ago he thought they were getting married in the spring. Now... He reached for his water glass, wishing it were something stronger.

"I have to rethink everything thanks to this deadline," Lori said as she pushed aside her menu. They were seated on the terrace at the Oyster Bay Hotel, where they were staying: him indefinitely; Lori, through the weekend. "I mean, they really sprang this on me."

"You could say that again," Nick muttered. Then, pouncing on her hesitation, he suggested, "Why don't you just tell them no? It's our wedding."

"But it's my job," Lori said, leaning forward. Her voice had risen a notch and there was a hardness in her eyes that told him she wasn't going to back down on this. Not that he expected her to. When she'd called to tell him they needed to push up the date, he knew better than to argue. As he told her, he'd learned it was easier to defer to her. She was the wedding expert, as she liked to point out.

"I'm in the business of weddings," Lori continued, another phrase that had been tossed around when he protested the change in date. He didn't bother to point out that she frequently referred to her job at the wedding magazine as a stepping stone, a launching pad for bigger things. The job had brought her back to New York from California, but the goal was always to get back into fashion, to get into something bigger and better.

He'd always admired her ambition. Now, as he took a sip of his beer, he told himself that he needed to remember this. That he needed to remember all the reasons that he fell in love with Lori in the first place.

"This wedding has to be perfect!" she said, rather aggressively, he thought.

Perfect. Another phrase he was growing a little tired of lately. He looked up, grateful that the waiter had approached. "Cheeseburger. Medium rare. And um, a shake. Chocolate."

"Whipped cream, sir?"

Nick could feel Lori's eyes boring through him. He kept his gaze firmly on the waiter. "Please."

He caught Lori staring at him across the table, wide-eyed. "He'll have the grilled cod, not the burger. I'll have the mixed green salad, dressing on the side. And sparkling water. For the table."

"And the shake?" The waiter's eyes flicked to him, and Nick sighed deeply.

"Just the water."

Lori gave him a wry look when the waiter walked away. "A cheeseburger, Nick? Our wedding is going to be on the cover of my magazine. We have an eight-page spread."

Nick set his jaw. There was no use arguing with Lori when she was like this, and now was certainly not the time, not when they were in a public setting. Still, he couldn't hold back completely.

"I told you that I would have preferred a spring wedding."

Her eyes narrowed a flash. "But then the wedding wouldn't be featured in the magazine."

He shrugged. "Would that really be so bad?"

"Yes, Nick! Yes, it would. Not everyone on staff gets their wedding featured. And a cover article—do you know how special that is?"

"I just think our wedding should be special enough," he pointed out.

Her eyes filled with tears, and for a moment, he felt like the biggest jerk in the world, until she hissed across the table, "This wedding is the most important opportunity of my career. Don't ruin it for me, Nick."

He stared at her across the table, wondering for not the first time since their engagement how all this had happened, how he was here, sitting across from a woman he was supposed to marry in one month's time. They had been in love—once. They'd grown up together. Spent holidays together. Heck, he knew her parents' house as well as his own. He played golf with her father. He shot hoops with her younger brother. He knew the exact brand of white wine her mother preferred, and he always brought her a bottle when they visited.

The Addisons were his family, and he hadn't even married into it yet.

This was all just nerves. Wedding jitters making her twitchy and tense. God knew he was guilty of suffering from them himself.

His phone vibrated on the table and he scanned the screen. His father. Normally he'd find an excuse to dodge the call, let it slip to voicemail, but right now he needed an excuse to end this conversation before he said something to Lori that he'd later come to regret.

"I should take this. It's about the buy-out," he explained.

She fluttered her fingers as she picked up her own phone. "Don't worry about it. I have some wedding things to think about anyway. Want me to have them send your lunch up to the room?"

He pushed back his chair and gave her a kiss on the cheek. "I'll let the waiter know."

He connected the call as he moved toward the service station, flagging down the waiter. "The cheeseburger," he said. "Can you send it up to the penthouse suite?"

The waiter gave him a small smile. "Not a problem, sir. And the shake?"

"Yes," Nick said. God, yes.

Already he felt better, if not a tad rebellious. He made a mental note of the waiter's name. A young kid, probably on break from college. He'd be sure to bring him back next year once he was owner of the establishment.

"Dad," he said into the receiver as he strode into the lobby, cool and refreshing and a sharp contrast from the humidity of the day, despite the breeze coming in off the ocean.

"I hear you're pushing up the wedding," his father ground out.

"Lori's pushing up the wedding," Nick clarified.

"And you're getting married at that hotel you're hell-bent on purchasing," his father said, seeming more disturbed by this than the sudden urgency of their nuptials. "Have you reconsidered my ideas on the renovation?"

Nick dropped into a chair in the lobby; the burger wouldn't be up for a while. It was a beautiful space, with high ceilings and tasteful décor in shades of blues and pops of greens. Sure, the navy carpet was fading in places and the white paint on the woodwork and trim was nicked and peeling, but there was an elegance to the space that couldn't be debated.

He loved this hotel. Loved the French doors and the terraces with the endless view of the sea. Loved the nostalgia of the colorful wallpaper that changed from room to room. He loved the tradition: the old-fashioned, oversized bar overlooking the pool. He even loved the lounge chairs, that were creaky and plastic, from another era.

From another time. A better time. A happier time.

If his father had his way, they'd strip out every inch of character and replace it with something modern and sleek.

Something generic.

"I'm not sure the town planning committee would go for that plan," he hedged.

"We wouldn't change the outside, just the inside. It's so old—"

"It's historic," Nick corrected him. "It's the kind of place that people remember. And it's in very good condition, I can promise you that. Besides, as I've said, I don't think we'll have a problem sprucing things up while maintaining the integrity of the original design."

"Is this about your mother?" his father suddenly said, and a long silence followed. Harold Tyler rarely spoke of his late wife. "Because she spent a few years in that town as a child?"

It was more than a few years, but Nick didn't see a point in arguing. Not now. Certainly not about his mother.

"You said that now was the time to start my own portfolio with the business, and that's what I'm doing," Nick said evenly.

"This doesn't fit the Tyler brand at all," Harold insisted. "You know what we do, Nick. We give people a new, fresh experience. People appreciate historic architecture, sure. But they want something new and exciting. Clean. Fresh. And they want to sleep on a good mattress."

Nick sighed. It was the same argument they'd had for months, ever since Nick pushed for the purchase of this hotel, seizing an opportunity to take on projects that were different from Tyler's usual properties.

"I'm going to have to ask you to trust me on this one," he said. "I have a meeting with a contractor again this week, and I think you'll be impressed with what we come up with."

"I don't see how that's possible from what you told me," his father said. "It's the twenty-first century. No one wants to stay in a hotel with a musty smell and a rundown elevator."

"I do," Nick said with a smile. He stood, his stomach grumbling at the anticipation of his cheeseburger, and crossed to the elevator, which was admittedly a little slow compared to the ones they featured in their other properties.

For a flicker of a second, he felt a creeping doubt, that maybe he wasn't making the right choice after all. That he should stick with what was tried and true, what they'd always done. What worked. That he should go back to New York, sit in his sterile corner office, and oversee the development of projects that left him cold.

He wouldn't risk failing. He wouldn't risk disappointment. It would be easier.

But he was tired of doing what was expected of him. He was the golden boy. The only son.

There were expectations.

And for a horrible moment that passed almost as quickly as he dared to register it, he thought of Lori.

Chapter Four

The only thing Chloe wanted to do tonight was go for a run (on the treadmill; *not* the park), shower, pour a glass of very cold white wine, and do what she always did when the stress got to her: clean. Of course, given that stress had been a part of her daily existence for practically forever, this meant that her apartment was already spotless; still, there was always a nook or cranny that might benefit from a little elbow grease. And she could always do another load of laundry. Maybe scrub down the stovetop. Tackle the bathroom tiles.

Melanie once asked if Chloe could give her the name of her cleaning lady, and Chloe had burst out laughing, but at least she knew that if Bayside Brides went belly up, she might just have a fallback. She really knew how to put a scrub brush to work. And a toothbrush, too, for those little hard to reach places.

But tonight, there would be no scrubbing the grout in her shower for relief. Tonight all the girls were getting together to welcome Hannah home from her honeymoon. There was no way out of it, and even the excuse of work (after all, the Addison wedding was looming, and quickly approaching) didn't seem good enough. Besides, she wouldn't have even had the Addison wedding if it weren't for Hannah. She needed to show up and thank her, even if the opportunity was starting to feel more like a curse than a blessing.

So, with a heavy sigh, she locked the door to the shop and joined Sarah and Melanie as they walked down Main Street, toward Coast, the newest restaurant to open in Oyster Bay as part of the expansion that was intended to revitalize Main Street, bring in more tourists and pump up the economy.

The very revitalization that had brought Nick here, she thought, fumbling to retrieve her sunglasses from their case.

Sarah and Melanie had already been to the new restaurant, and had only good things to say about the drinks and ambience. "See, and you were all worried about new businesses coming into town," Melanie said.

Chloe didn't deny it. Change was always difficult for her. Routine was comforting. But Melanie was the opposite, happy to take risks, willing to try new things. And sometimes she was right. After all, it was Melanie who had pushed for them to expand their business from a retail store to a full-service wedding business. And look where that had gotten them.

A cover story with *Here Comes the Bride* magazine.

The Addison wedding.

A month of hell ahead of her as she watched the man she had dared to feel something for plan his wedding to another woman.

Her tread was nearly as heavy as the weight in her chest as she walked beside her cousin, barely catching half of their conversation. Just this morning life had felt full of hope and anticipation. Life had never felt better. A cover article. National exposure. The possibility of Nick calling her for a date.

She should have known that it would all come crashing down. That it was, quite simply, too good to be true.

She mustered up a smile as they walked onto the patio of the new restaurant, which was crowded and lively, with energetic music playing through speakers and strings of lights draped over dozens of bistro tables and rattan armchairs and sofas. Hannah and her sisters were already seated on a grouping of couches, joined by the Harper sisters, the six cousins holding glasses of wine that appeared to have just been poured.

The Bayside women joined the others, giving air kisses and admiring Hannah's tan, and asking all the details of her trip. It had been a short honeymoon, because of Dan's eleven-year-old daughter Lucy, who had stayed with her mother during the week that Dan and Hannah were away.

"So, do you feel any different, being a married woman?" Sarah asked eagerly as she dropped onto a seat.

"Gathering research?" Hannah's cousin, Abby, chided Sarah. It was no surprise that now that Sarah was dating Chris Foster, the owner of the estate where Hannah's wedding had been held, it was obvious that she had wedding fever again, but then, Sarah had always had wedding fever—it was one of the reasons that Chloe had hired her. She was passionate. She believed in love.

Chloe had always thought she believed in love too. She just hadn't considered it for herself. Until Nick.

She stiffened and placed an order for whatever the others were drinking, trying to relax into the evening while all the unmarried yet not single women at the table bantered over who would be the next one to walk down the aisle.

Chloe's money was on the obvious soul mates Melanie and Jason, if she were a betting woman, which she wasn't, because betting was far too risky for her comfort level. After all, Hannah's youngest sister, Kelly, had uprooted her life when she found love in Oyster Bay, and their middle sister Evie had been with Liam for about a year now. It could be any of them next. There was no predicting it.

Love, much like life, couldn't be planned.

And that was why she had always done her best to avoid it. Until now.

"Although the person who should really be thinking about a wedding is Chloe," said Hannah's youngest sister, Kelly.

Bridget, the eldest of the Harper sisters frowned. "Because she's a wedding planner?"

"Because she caught the bouquet!" Kelly reminded everyone.

"More like got hit by the bouquet," Chloe muttered. Her drink had arrived. She took a long sip, hoping that by the time she came up for air that the topic would be dropped and she wouldn't have to be reminded of the bouquet, that night, or Nick.

"Who was that man who caught you?" Abby asked, her eyes flashing with interest that Chloe was oh so eager to shut down. Immediately.

But Hannah cut in, saying, "Oh, he's a client of Dan's. A big one, actually. He's a hotel developer and apparently they're in talks to buy the Oyster Bay Hotel."

"Well, he was pretty cute," Abby continued. Her eyebrows waggled in Chloe's direction. Chloe fluttered her lashes.

"If you're thinking I should be interested—"

"Why not? You should make more time for fun," Abby continued. "Everything can't be all business all the time."

"Actually, it can be." Chloe set her glass on the table. "Nick is engaged. And his fiancée is a client."

For now. The thought curdled in her stomach. There was no telling if her connection to the groom would be revealed and the business would be taken elsewhere. Or if Nick would feel uncomfortable, maybe even a little shady, and suggest to Lori that they use her connection back in New York instead, plan things from a distance.

"Lori Addison," Melanie cut in excitedly. "She's an editor at *Here Comes the Bride* magazine. She saw the pictures from Hannah's wedding and decided to have her wedding here in Oyster Bay. Of course, Nick taking over the hotel probably added to the decision."

"Probably," Chloe said. She glanced up, noticing that everyone was staring at her with curiosity, no doubt wondering why she wasn't matching Melanie's enthusiasm. She sat up a little straighter. Really, she needed to snap out of this. Since when did anything get in the way of her career? Never. It came first and foremost, always. And good things were happening. She just needed to focus on that. "She's going to have her wedding featured as the center story of the country weddings issue."

"The *cover* story!" Sarah chimed in, her eyes wistful.

"What an amazing opportunity!" Evie looked impressed.

"Well, it's all thanks to Hannah," Chloe said, managing a grateful smile. After all, she should be thankful. A magazine cover—heck, any mention in a magazine—was a huge opportunity. None of that should be overshadowed by the identity of the groom.

"You have nothing to thank me for," Hannah said.

"You planned a beautiful wedding and Lori noticed that. She's not exactly easy to please."

Wonderful, Chloe thought, taking another sip of her drink.

Margo Harper held up her glass of white wine. "I think this calls for a toast. To Bayside Brides being put on the map."

Chloe clinked glasses with the girls, wishing that she could drum up more enthusiasm than she felt.

Melanie elbowed her when the conversation switched back to Hannah's trip. "You don't seem very excited."

"Just anxious," Chloe gave a tight smile. "You know me. I'll be relieved when it's over."

"Well, don't wish it away. This is what you wanted. What you worked hard for! Enjoy it."

Enjoy it. She knew her cousin was right, that she had worked hard for this. So, so hard. She had dedicated her entire life to building up the business, took a risk by expanding it, even when that left uncertainty on the table. Landing a client like Lori Addison was more than she could have ever wished for. She should be pinching herself, and she wanted to. She wanted to wake up, realize that none of this had even happened.

When did a dream turn into a nightmare?

Oh, right. When she went and fell for the groom.

*

Nick glanced at his watch with growing impatience. Lori had said she'd meet him in the lobby at seven, and now it was nearly half past the hour. He was just about to text her, again, when the elevator doors slid open and she emerged, looking like she was going out to eat on Park Avenue rather than downtown Oyster Bay.

"Those elevators move at a glacial speed!" she tutted as he stood to greet her. "Honestly, are you sure you want to invest in this place? Wouldn't it be better to build new?"

"On what land?" he pointed out. Ocean-front space was tight and the price was steep. "This place has good bones. And it's a good investment. Look at all the people."

"What about the Vineyard? Or Nantucket?" Lori said, not for the first time.

"I've explained all that," he said, tension building in his tone. "There may be opportunities in those places down the road, but right now, this is where I'm starting my portfolio."

His portfolio. He still couldn't quite believe it. For so many years he'd toed the line, lived in his father's shadow, all the while knowing that it would pay off when he took over the business someday, when he could finally take on projects he was passionate about, that made all the other stuff worthwhile. Now his father was winding down. Change was coming, whether Harold liked it or not. And even though Nick planned to preserve most of what he'd learned from his father over the years, he was ready to move things in a different direction.

"Besides," Nick said. "You were the one who said it was serendipitous that the country weddings issue needed a cover story. We could always wait. Get married in the city."

She eyed him. They both knew that Lori wasn't going to pass up this opportunity.

She didn't look convinced as she glanced around the lobby. "I guess this will work. But I wish we could have had those elevators fixed before our wedding."

"About the wedding…" he began. He needed to bring up Chloe, that they'd met, maybe even suggest they go with a different wedding planner. It would be easier that way. Less…complicated. Then he could focus on Lori. The wedding.

His stomach rumbled. He needed some food. Something delicious. He hoped the portions at the restaurant were generous.

But before he could finish, she linked her arm through his and said, "Can we discuss this at the restaurant? I'm hoping the food is better than my lunch. I'll have to make sure Chloe speaks with the chef so he understands our expectations for the wedding."

"About the wedding," Nick said again. He braced himself for a backlash, wondered where to begin the conversation. There was no easy way. "I hadn't expected it to come up so quickly. It wasn't what we planned."

"Well, my plans changed," she said simply. "Our families understand. And none of our friends would miss it, of course. They can come up for the weekend. I'm sure the hotel can clear out rooms for such a big event."

In other words, cancel other people's reservations.

He blinked, tried to get back on track.

"It's just that I had planned to be in Oyster Bay for a while. For work. If we're going to buy this property, I need to know that all my construction plans can be put in place. I'm not able to get back to Manhattan much this month."

"That's okay," she said to his surprise.

He glanced at her as she dropped his arm to push through the revolving door onto the sidewalk. When they were outside, he said, "You won't mind being apart?"

"Our careers are important to us, Nick," she said simply. "It's what brought us together."

"Well, that and our parents," he said wryly, but she gave him a sharp look. After all, Harold and Chess went way back, to their college days at Yale.

"You're not in this for the wrong reason, are you?" Lori asked.

She was posing the exact question he had wanted to ask her, from the moment she brought up the topic of marriage, to the timing of her wanting to announce their engagement at her office summer party, when she knew a cover story was needed for the country weddings issue.

But then he thought back to happier times. Before the wedding talk began. Before she started focusing on dresses and her coworkers, and what they might think. Maybe Lori was right. They were both career driven.

That's all it was.

But the strange feeling that twisted his gut left him uneasy.

"Where to tonight?" he asked. Last night they had planned to go into town and ended up with room service, staring at their laptops while they ate in silence. Salad. He'd picked at his, excused himself to the ice machine and ordered four candy bars from the vending machine that he'd shoveled down while standing in the hallway.

But it was Saturday, and they always went out for dinner on Saturday nights. It was a tradition. They had traditions, he reminded himself. Like a normal couple.

Really, he was just getting jitters.

"Well, what options do we have?" Lori didn't look amused as they walked down Main Street. "Honestly, if it wasn't for an oceanfront wedding, I don't think this is the location I would have chosen for the cover story. I'd much prefer the Ritz, or a Tyler property, of course," she quickly said.

More like a different Tyler hotel. One that fit her idea of status. He eyed her, not liking her wording, but decided not to read into it. Besides, he had bigger issues to address.

"I'm buying that hotel," he reminded her. "You know how I feel about this project."

"Oh, I know, honey," she said, again slipping her arm through his. "And see, it all worked out. Cover issue. Beachfront wedding. You don't hear me complaining!" She pointed to a restaurant at the end of the next block, with an outdoor patio that appeared to wrap around the corner. "Let's go there. It seems popular."

His spirits lifted as they approached. The menu posted outside the front door met Lori's approval, as did the ambience. The night, it seemed, was saved.

He felt his shoulders relax for the first time all day, until he saw her, in a corner of the patio, and something strange kicked up inside him again. Chloe. Their wedding planner.

"This place is crowded," he said quickly. "Let's try the next one."

"This place is perfect," Lori insisted, as he knew she would. Because it did seem perfect. Lively, fun, vibrant.

But unlike Lori, he'd never sought perfection. He just sought...something more, he thought, as he turned his back to the table of women in the corner.

*

Hannah was showing them photos of Tuscany on her camera, a huge and expensive thing that she was rarely without, when Sarah said, "Hey. Isn't that Lori? The new client?"

Chloe felt her heart drop into her stomach. "What? Where?"

Her eyes flicked over the patio, hoping that Sarah was wrong, hoping that if Lori was here, that she was at least alone.

"There. Near the bar. It is. The big clients!"

Clients. Well, there it was. Chloe's mouth felt dry as she spotted them, at a table at the other end of the patio. Lori looked incredibly chic in a black linen romper and gold sandals. Of course she was engaged to a man like Nick. They looked like something out of a magazine. Him in his khaki shorts and loose white linen shirt rolled at the sleeves, his hair slightly rumpled. They had a bottle of wine between them, chilling in an ice bucket in the center of their table. They'd probably share a selection of the small plates, too. They were chic. Effortless. They looked like they were made for each other.

She looked away before one of them felt her stare.

"Small world," she said to Sarah. More like small town, she thought to herself. That was the trouble with Oyster Bay, wasn't it? You couldn't escape if you needed to. She reached for her handbag, which was resting at her feet. "You know, I don't feel like talking shop tonight," she whispered to Sarah. "I'll probably head out—"

But it was too late. Hannah whooped at the sight of her friend and called out to Lori, and now Lori was looking around. And now her hand was in the air. And damn it, she was waving.

Chloe's stomach pooled with dread.

"That's Lori and Nick," Melanie explained to the others, as all three women from Bayside Brides waved back. Chloe patted at her face to make sure she was still wearing her sunglasses, knowing that she couldn't quite bring her eyes to match her tense smile.

"The man who saved you?" Bridget asked.

"Well, I wouldn't say he—"

"He's cute!" Abby said, a grin spreading over her mouth.

Cute. Yes. But taken. A little fact he had failed to mention in their not one, but two interactions.

Chloe thought back to that walk around the pond and felt so disappointed that she had to reach for her wine glass.

"Lori!" Hannah called again as Lori walked to their table, Nick a few feet behind.

"Please don't mention the bouquet hitting me," Chloe pleaded with her friends. She couldn't stand to think about it anymore, and she certainly didn't need it coming up now, when it hadn't been mentioned this morning in the meeting.

Hannah stood up and greeted her old friend with a long hug and soon both were talking over the other so quickly that Chloe couldn't make sense of half of what they were saying, and it didn't appear they intended to stop anytime soon. That was confirmed when Hannah said, "Tell the waiter to bring your drinks over here. We can make room."

Oh, no. No. Chloe looked up, catching Nick's eye. He hovered behind Lori, his hands in his pockets, looking just as out of place as she felt. A hundred thoughts seemed to pass silently between them, but she couldn't read a single one.

"Here, move down everyone," Hannah said, as she

pulled Lori onto the seat beside her, and then they were all shifting to the side, making room for two more. Chloe was careful to keep her body pressed tight to Sarah's and Hannah's, but as luck would have it, she ended up facing Nick.

"So Nick, I hear it's your turn next." Margo smiled good-naturedly. She had no reason to be anything but generous right now, after all.

"Appears so." Nick looked uncomfortable as he glanced at the women.

Chloe narrowed her eyes. A strange response to a direct question. Shy? Possibly. Guilty? Likely. Cold feet? Obviously. She saw it all the time. With brides. With grooms. Even with the parents of the engaged couple.

"And you're getting married at the Oyster Bay Hotel?" Bridget had a vested interest in the question, Chloe knew. After all, she might end up accommodating some out of town guests—if she had any cancellations before then.

"Maybe," Lori surprised Chloe by saying.

She nearly dropped the wine glass she was holding in her hand, and cut a glance across the table to Nick, who looked just as shocked as she felt.

"What do you mean?" he said in a low voice.

"Well, Hannah's wedding was just so lovely. And like the hotel, it was beachfront. But maybe a little more…special?"

Oh. Well, that was a relief. For a minute there, Chloe thought she had changed her mind about holding her wedding here in town.

But Nick didn't look satisfied. He stared at Lori. Actually, it was more of a glare.

"You wouldn't mind, would you, Hannah?"

Hannah looked mildly put out, but Chloe knew her well enough to know she wouldn't protest. "Of course not. You should have the wedding of your dreams, Lori."

"That's what I've been telling Nick," Lori said, leaning over to squeeze Nick's hand.

Chloe looked away, feeling uncomfortable, even though she shouldn't. They were a couple. Nick was in a relationship with Lori. They were getting married.

And she was helping them.

She stayed for one more drink, avoiding eye contact, letting Lori and Hannah catch up and reminisce about their days at the magazine, listening to Nick ask the other women about what they did, how long they'd lived here, asking about spots in town.

He was a friendly guy, that's all he was. But tonight, he was decidedly unfriendly with her. She met his eye, a few times, and looked away, unable to join in the conversation, and maybe, unwilling.

She gathered up her bag, hoping she could slip away without any need for suspicion or explanation.

"Leaving so soon?" Evie asked, looking disappointed.

"I've got a big wedding to plan," she said, managing a smile.

Melanie frowned at her as she stood, and then looked down at Nick, something flickering in her eyes as Chloe walked away from the table.

Perhaps her ever observant cousin had noticed that Chloe had said goodbye to everyone but the groom.

Chapter Five

The shop was quiet for a weekend afternoon. So quiet that Chloe may have been concerned, except for the fact that the morning had brought in three walk-ins, one resulting in a sale of a pair of satin heels with a crystal broach clip, and a bespoke jewelry set made by local artisan Beth Sanders, sold exclusively to Bayside Brides—Chloe had made sure of that when she'd seen how good Beth's work was.

And it was summer. A sunny afternoon that probably called more for beach time than shopping. No doubt as the afternoon winded down, people would pack up their towels and coolers and take a stroll on Main Street before the shops closed. Summer was always their busiest season. So busy that more and more, all three women on staff at the shop found themselves working even when they weren't scheduled. Even if they weren't manning the storefront, Melanie was often running off to do a fitting for a custom dress order, and Chloe was often visiting venues with excited brides. Business was booming, and even with Sarah's help, they were spread thin.

Chloe chewed her lip. Technically the business was strong. They were growing. They had seen a profit every year since the first year, which Chloe had factored into her business plan. She had a comfortable life: an apartment that was small but that suited her. She had no intention of moving, no need for anything larger. She didn't travel—who had the time?

And traveling alone…well, it wasn't exactly appealing to her.

Meaning, really, maybe she didn't *need* to take on the Addison-Tyler after all. The thought of saying she was too busy, too pressed for time with the new date, made her feel more relaxed than she had felt since the time that she thought they had ordered the wrong color of bridesmaid dresses for Callie Parkinson's wedding and it turned out that they hadn't, of course they hadn't. Chloe never mistakes. Except for Nick.

"That was fun last night," Sarah said to her as she steamed the front of a gown that had just been unboxed. It was a beautiful ballgown, part of their fall line, in a creamy ivory with a lace overlay and buttons all up the back.

Come September, it would go in their front window.

Really, September was just around the corner. So why

did this month suddenly feel so long and yet short, all at the same time?

Chloe looked down at her calendar, considering the week ahead. A few fittings, a few second fittings, a prospect for a wedding next summer, and a meeting for a holiday wedding that had her particularly excited. By August, it was always like this. The summer was wonderful, but she was ready for a change of pace. For snow to grace the sidewalks and frock the tree branches. For the quiet that only winter could seem to bring to Oyster Bay.

"I think that Lori and Nick really like you," Sarah remarked, and Chloe looked up sharply. Had Sarah picked up on anything between her and the groom? Or had it all been in Chloe's head?

She had to think it was the latter. The man was getting married. He was planning his wedding. In a month he would be a husband to Lori Addison.

And she really needed to stop thinking that there was any sort of connection between them. He was just a friendly guy… And she, well, she was a little lonely, she supposed.

"I'm not sure I should keep the business," she heard herself say. There, she'd said it. It felt bold. Uncharacteristic. And the horror in Sarah's face proved it.

"Not keep the business?" Sarah exclaimed. "Are you crazy? The wedding is going to be on the cover of *Here Comes the Bride* magazine." She jammed her finger against one of several issues that they kept fanned out on the table in the seating area. "Think of the exposure! Everyone on the East Coast will want a wedding like that. You're going to put Oyster Bay and Bayside Brides on the map."

Chloe swallowed hard. She knew it was true. All of it was true. Maybe she just needed a reminder. "You're right. I guess I just panicked with the timing. A month isn't a lot of time to plan something this big."

"You can do it," Sarah said cheerfully as she walked toward the dressing rooms. "Keep your eye on the prize."

Eye on the prize. Chloe would do just that. It was better than keeping an eye from wandering back to Nick and that lopsided grin and those warm eyes that seemed to hold hers a second longer than they should every time they met.

"I'm running out to lunch." Sarah emerged from the dressing room with three veils that had been rejected at Chloe's appointment this morning. The bride was picky. Very picky. And Chloe had seen her share of picky brides in the seven years since she'd opened the shop. Still, she got it. After all, some might say that she was picky herself. "Want me to bring you back something?"

It had always been rare for Chloe to take a real lunch break. Usually she worked through, or dashed across Main Street to Angie's for a sandwich that she'd bring back and often forget about.

It wasn't like her to let her personal needs or desires interfere with anything related to her business.

"Thanks, but I think I'll grab something later." She opened her appointment book and considered her schedule for the week ahead. A first appointment tomorrow, meaning the bride would try on fifteen dresses and love them all. Or hate them all. A final fitting, which would hopefully be quick. And a menu tasting with Samantha King, who had already asked Melanie to redesign her custom gown at least four different times.

There would be no wishy-washiness over the menu if Chloe had any say.

The wedding bells that hung from the door jangled and Chloe looked up in anticipation of a customer, but it was just Melanie, returning from lunch.

It was immediately obvious that something was wrong. Very wrong. Chloe rolled through the possibilities. A fight with her boyfriend, Jason? Impossible. Jason and Melanie had been best friends all their lives before their relationship had developed into something more. A squabble with her mother? But that rarely happened, especially now that Melanie had finally settled down, putting Chloe's aunt's worry about her daughter at ease.

Nothing could be wrong with Melanie's personal life. And that only left one possibility.

Chloe closed her appointment book and gave Melanie her full attention, bracing herself for the worst. It was what she always did, even though she didn't want to, even though a lot of time people—especially her cousin Melanie—told her to relax. But Chloe didn't know how to relax. When you relaxed, you slipped. You set yourself up for failure. For disappointment. You had to keep your eyes open. Your guard up. You had to be careful.

She'd lost sight of that this week.

"What's wrong?" She realized that she was holding her breath.

Melanie winced. "Maybe you should have this first." She tried to hand Chloe a cookie. It was warm; Chloe could tell by the melting chocolate chips. But Chloe just shook her head. Melanie knew that an oversized—albeit delicious—cookie didn't fit Chloe's health regimen.

Besides, she was suddenly too anxious to even think about eating. Her stomach felt tight and her throat felt scratchy. It was the exact same way she'd felt growing up, when her father came home from work earlier than expected and she knew, because by then she had seen it enough times, that he was once again out of a job. That there wouldn't be a birthday party this year, maybe not even a present. That her lunches would get downgraded to jelly and bread sandwiches. That her mother would get a pinched look about her again.

That there was nothing Chloe could do to help. Not even herself.

Being a business owner was supposed to erase those fears. She was in control. She couldn't be fired. If a client decided they didn't want her services anymore, then she could make an extra effort to find another.

Only looking at Melanie's expression right now, she wondered if that was all wishful thinking. After all, owning your own business meant that you risked losing it too. And if that happened…

Then she'd have nothing.

"What is it?" Her heart was pounding and her jaw was so tight that she could feel the pain in her ears.

Melanie hesitated. "I know I told you not to worry about the Main Street expansion."

Chloe felt a "but" coming on. Of course she did. She alone had worried what expanding the business district of Oyster Bay could mean to Bayside Brides. Melanie had told her not to worry, that it would be good for their business, but Chloe couldn't help but worry. It was Chloe's job to worry.

"I saw a sign going up," Melanie said. She bit her lip. Here it came. "For an event planning company. Now, they didn't—"

But Chloe didn't hear anything more. Her blood was rushing so hard she could feel it in her ears. And event planning company. Just when she'd dared to agree to finally expand their business from a wedding gown boutique to a full-service wedding business.

"We're ruined," Chloe said. Well, not completely, but the wedding planning…it was what Chloe had really always wanted to do, not just sell dresses and veils and shoes. And now that she had a taste for it, she couldn't imagine going back. She loved seeing a wedding day through from start to finish, knowing that every last detail was taken into consideration. Back when she was just running the storefront, she had to bite her tongue to keep from voicing an opinion when a bride selected a flower girl dress that didn't match the flowers, or casually showed her an invitation in a font that was far too formal for the description of the event. It was so satisfying to now know that each of her brides were taken care of, and that she had played a part in giving them the wedding of their dreams.

The increase in her take-home pay had been a nice perk, too. All of it was set aside in a high-interest savings account, of course. Just in case...

And now that time had come. Would she need to tap into it? Just to get by?

"They didn't specifically say they did weddings, but..." The cousins exchanged a look.

"Of course they do weddings. It's not like there's a ton of corporate events to plan around here." Chloe sighed and grabbed her handbag that was in the cabinet under the counter. "I need to see this for myself."

"Take the full-hour break today," Melanie said gently. She switched places with Chloe and looked down at the appointment book. "It's slow today."

Somehow that no longer seemed like such a good thing. Chloe had gotten comfortable. Something she'd promised never to do. She should have known better. Just when you thought you were safe...Well, you weren't.

"I can't take a break. I have to meet clients."

Melanie's face perked up. "Of course! The Addison wedding! See? It's all going to be fine. The cover of a magazine, Chloe. We can display it all over the shop. Frame each page of the article."

Chloe felt a headache coming on. She hadn't even considered this, but of course it made sense. Why wouldn't they frame the article, boast their success? Then every customer who came into the shop would see how great they were, and Chloe would be able to stare at photos of Nick hand-feeding Lori cake every damn day.

Sarah was already returning with a brown bag, and Chloe managed to smile at her as she pushed into the shop and then stepped outside into the warm sunshine. Even the sunny summer day couldn't lift her spirits. Usually she enjoyed walking down Main Street, checking out the store windows or the flower pots that flanked each shop door. But today her eyes darted, scanning for the sign that Melanie had mentioned, part of the expansion of the business district toward the southern edge of town, all the way down toward The Lantern, an institution for locals and the best lobster salad in the state, if anyone asked her, which served as its caboose.

She came upon the sign quickly. It was cute. Too cute. Peony pink in an elegant, feminine scroll. In other words, it would be stiff competition. She scanned the details that were on display in the window. Opening this month. (Her palms began to sweat.) Tending to all personal events. (She was aware that she was actually panting now.) One-stop shop.

Oh, this was not good. Not good at all.

She stepped back, afraid of looking too interested, of drawing attention to herself. To this new business. She looked back up the street, at her own sweet shop which now seemed stale in comparison. It was classic, but it was hardly fresh and new. And people liked fresh and new.

Her heart was now beating so loudly that she saw no alternative. She would hit the treadmill. She would run. Run off her anxiety. Run until she wasn't panicking anymore. Until she was able to think clearly. With any luck, develop a strategy.

But first, she would meet Lori and Nick at the Oyster Bay Hotel. She had no choice.

*

To her great relief, Chloe found Lori alone in the lobby, tapping at her phone with impressive speed.

"Is Nick not joining us today?" She noted the hope in her tone and prayed that Lori hadn't picked up on it.

"He said he was going to look at some of the meeting rooms." Lori sighed audibly. "He really intends to buy this place."

Chloe wasn't sure what she was expected to say to that, but Lori didn't seem to be looking for a reply. Instead, she dropped her phone into her oversized handbag and pulled Chloe aside by the elbow.

"Listen, what are your thoughts about having the wedding at that exquisite mansion where Hannah had hers? Normally I'd want something more unique, of course, but the photos she showed me were stunning and it just…well, it called to me."

Chloe nodded. Crestview Manor was a stunning property, but she also knew that Sarah had gone to great lengths to secure the venue for Hannah when her original location had been cancelled due to flooding.

"I can certainly speak with the owner," she said. After all, Chris Foster was a very nice guy. And he had enjoyed himself at Hannah's wedding, if the fact that Sarah could hardly peel him from the dance floor said anything.

"Ask the owner about what?" a deep voice behind her made Chloe jump.

Lori looked up nervously. "Nick. I was just asking Chloe about Crestview Manor."

"We discussed this." His eyes were stony when he looked at Lori.

"You yourself said how beautiful that location was," Lori pointed out. "I hardly see why we have to have the wedding here, just because it's a property you intend to buy."

The Oyster Bay Hotel was beautiful, an icon to the town, adored by all, and stunning in its architecture, not to mention its sweeping seaside location. Normally, Chloe would stay out of these sorts of tiffs, but here she was siding with the bride. After all, she couldn't exactly side with Nick, could she? An engaged man who had never alluded to such?

"I can speak with Chris Foster today," she told the couple. "My colleague, Sarah Preston, has a personal relationship with the owner and may be able to give some insight."

Lori's face lit up. "Thank you!"

Chloe skirted a look at Nick. He looked far from thrilled. "Well, we're here. Should we take a tour? I'm happy to share how other brides have used the space."

Chloe hitched her handbag higher on her shoulder and the women followed Nick, letting him lead them through the lobby and out onto the back patio, which was currently set up for lunch. Chloe knew the property, knew it well. She'd attended many events here over the years and it was a stunning location, an Oyster Bay landmark, really, and she felt the need to do it justice, even if Lori seemed to have other ideas in mind.

"The Garden Terrace is a lovely location for a rehearsal dinner if you wanted to keep everything on the property," she said, motioning to a set of French doors that led out to the space.

Nick gave her a little smile. "It's one of my favorite parts of the hotel, actually."

An eye roll came from Lori. "Every part of this hotel is your favorite, Nick." But she covered the slight with a playful grin.

Nick's smile faltered when he caught Chloe's eye, and Chloe frowned. There was obvious tension between the bride and groom, not that she'd be reading too far into it. After all, weddings were stressful. Some of the worst arguments took place in the weeks leading up to the wedding. Surely, this was just more of the same.

"Why don't we go onto the terrace and walk down to the beach, since that's where the ceremony and reception will take place?" Chloe said, taking control of the situation just as she would have done with any other clients. "We have a few options when it comes to set up."

She kept her eyes straight ahead as they moved outside and into the warm sunshine. The tide was coming in and she could see the waves gaining strength even from this distance from the shoreline. For a moment, all felt right with the world, just like it always did, when she was a kid and she'd run out to the beach, toss shells into the water, wondering where they would end up.

The ocean was constant. Little else in her world ever was.

"Well, ideally, the ceremony would be held down at the shoreline. In the event of bad weather—"

"Oh, *no*. Not an option." Lori was shaking her head as if she had a vote in such a thing.

Chloe resisted the urge to exchange a look with Nick, but she could feel him watching her.

"Tents can be brought in."

"Tents don't make the cover of a magazine," Lori explained. "Neither do storm clouds. Bad lighting," she added.

Chloe felt her jaw pulse. No, she didn't imagine that tents would make the cover of the magazine. And then what? No cover story meant less publicity. And wasn't that the entire reason she was planning this wedding?

She caught Nick looking at her. His eyes widened ever so slightly, as if it to let her know that he got it, that he was on her side.

She pushed away the flutter in her stomach and cleared her throat.

"Well, it's unlikely there will be rain, at least not all day, but just in case, know that I'll prepare for it. And you're not the only bride to worry about this. But even in the event of a shower, I've learned that little can dampen a wedding day. It will be the happiest day of your life, regardless." She slanted a glance at Nick as she pressed her lips together.

"Not if it rains," Lori insisted. Her cheeks were growing pink as her voice rose. "This has to be the most *perfect* day of my life." She glanced up at Nick. "Of our lives," she corrected herself.

"Can we find a word other than perfect?" Nick asked, and Chloe swallowed a smile. She'd used that word a hundred times before, but more and more, the implied pressure felt draining and worrisome. Yes, the wedding would be perfect if she had anything to do with it, but was it really all about a table centerpiece and a three-tiered cake? These things might be important to her as the planner, but it should be about so much more to the bride.

"The wedding will be beautiful," Chloe assured her. In many ways, it would be the wedding she always wished she could have had.

Right down to the groom, she thought, kicking herself.

Lori huffed out a breath and wrinkled her nose as she looked around the veranda. "It is a beautiful space," she agreed, almost reluctantly. "And I can see where it fits the theme of the issue. Country weddings. This hotel certainly feels…rustic."

Rustic wasn't exactly the description that Chloe would use. With its cedar siding and whaler's watch tower, it was more historic than anything else. Coastal, nautical. Not rustic.

"It's a special property," she said. "And it certainly has an ambience that is quintessential to Oyster Bay. Imagine the flowers. The tables set up on that side there. The lighthouse in the distance. It's a true escape for your readers."

She frowned at her own choice of wording. Was she pitching a story here or planning a wedding? The two were becoming jumbled.

"And it is a property that I'll be buying. That we'll own," Nick stressed.

"So now it's all about your career now, hmm?" Lori gave him a long look and then shrugged her shoulders. "But you're right, Chloe. It certainly fits the image that I was hoping to convey."

This was all becoming weird, and Chloe decided to shift focus back to the details she was more familiar with. "You said you already have a dress. Can you send me some photos when you have a chance? It will help me with making suggestions for the bridesmaid dresses."

Lori tapped at her phone. "Just making a memo. Oh. An email. Oh, are you kidding me? They've moved up our fall shoot to ten tomorrow. That means I'll need to fly out today instead of tomorrow." She darted a glance at Chloe.

"It will be okay," Chloe was quick to reply. "We'll stay in touch all week, and that will give me time to gather up more options to present to you next weekend. And the only other item we had on the agenda today was to go over the menu."

"And I can take care of that," Nick said.

Lori gave him a wry look. "Well," she said, addressing Chloe. "I'd first like to know about Crestview. But I suppose there's no harm in letting Nick sample the menu."

"Well, we should nail a few things down today." Chloe didn't need to point out the obvious, that the wedding was now less than a month away. "If I could get a color for the bridesmaids, then I could email you some dress options and get those ordered. It would also help me to pull together some flower ideas."

"Pink," Lori said.

"Any particular shade?" Chloe asked.

"Blush," Lori said. "It's elegant. And it will look good on the cover."

If Chloe didn't know better, she would say that Lori cared more about the cover photo than even Chloe did.

"I'll text you the measurements of my wedding party once we decide on a style," Lori said as she tapped at her phone and moved back into the lobby. "And for anything urgent, just ask Nick. He knows me so well that I'm sure he could tell you exactly what I want. You don't mind, do you, Nick?"

He looked momentarily rattled. "Not at all."

"Perfect." Lori grinned as she looped her arm through his.

Chloe pursed her lips. Perfect. This wedding was getting just more perfect by the day.

Chapter Six

Nick woke the next morning with a strange feeling that a weight had been lifted. He pulled back the curtains, looking out onto the Atlantic, wondering if it was the sun, or the meeting he had lined up with Dan to go over the renovation plans for the hotel that had him in better spirits.

But he had a sinking feeling that his mood stemmed from Lori's return to New York.

She was just wound up, he told himself as he took the elevator down to the lobby. Engaged women got this way. There were entire television shows devoted to it. And she wasn't that bad, not really. She just wanted the wedding to be beautiful. Little girls dreamed about that sort of thing. He should want her to have the day of her dreams. He shouldn't still be annoyed that she had even mentioned having their wedding at Crestview instead of here at the hotel.

He'd talk to Chloe, he decided. Surely, she would understand.

But then again, he thought, remembering the way she refused to so much as meet his eye yesterday, maybe she wouldn't. Maybe she didn't like him, even though he'd hoped that they could be friends.

After all, if he had anything to do with it, he'd be spending a lot of time here in Oyster Bay. He wouldn't even be opposed to staying here for large chunks of the year, buy a seasonal home for summers and holidays, but something told him that Lori wouldn't agree with that. She'd need him back in New York. Need him to accompany her to the endless list of charity events that seemed to dot their calendar. Small-town life wasn't her thing. He still couldn't quite get past his shock when she'd suggested a country wedding. But then, the chance to be on a magazine cover made it worthwhile to her, he supposed.

She was a city girl, always was and always would be. And he was…ready for a change.

He frowned at that thought as the elevator deposited him into the lobby. He checked his watch. Right on time. Dan was already waiting for him in the main dining room, where they would discuss his preliminary budget and ideas.

Nick waved and joined him at a table near the window.

Most of the patrons had elected for outside tables, but Dan explained, "I thought we'd have fewer interruptions here."

"Absolutely," Nick agreed. He turned over the coffee mug and sat back as the waiter filled it. "I'm all about discretion."

"How are the negotiations going?" Dan asked. He opened a thick folder and handed Nick a stapled set of papers.

"Friendly. The owner of the hotel is eager to sell and I'm eager to buy."

"Sounds like a perfect match." Dan grinned.

A perfect match. That was a familiar statement, and one he'd heard all too often lately. He suspected he would hear it again, as the wedding approached.

"Nothing is perfect," he said a little tightly, as he reached for the menu. Then, hating himself for letting his personal feelings creep into his professional life, he held up a hand. "Sorry. It's the wedding planning. I swear, if I hear the word *perfect* one more time..."

Dan laughed. "Hate to break it to you, but you can probably bet on it."

"How'd you get through it?" Nick asked. He didn't know Dan, not yet really, but he felt a connection with the guy, as a newly married man to one that would soon be. Hannah and Lori went back as old friends. They'd be a couple to socialize with, and something told him that he and Dan were going to be fast friends.

Maybe it would be enough to keep Lori interested in

the town.

But he had a feeling that was wishful thinking on his part.

The waiter returned to take their order and Nick didn't hold back. "I'll take the Oyster Bay special and a biscuit with jam. And the blueberry pancakes."

The waiter hesitated. "The special comes with toast. Would you like the biscuit instead?"

"I'll take both," Nick said, aware of Dan's eyes on him. He was fully aware that the special included scrambled eggs, bacon, sausage, toast, a side of fruit, and hash browns. "I figure I should sample the menu if I'm going to be buying the place," he said to cover up his embarrassment, but he had the sense that Dan could care less about appearances. He was a decent guy. Hard working. Real.

"This wasn't my first wedding, actually," Dan said when the waiter left the table. "But it was easier this time. It's different when you're marrying for the right reasons."

Nick picked up his coffee mug and took a long sip. For the right reason. And what was that? True love, he supposed. But could it ever really be that simple?

He looked at Dan, who seemed completely at peace as he flicked through the paperwork they were yet to discuss. He supposed it could be.

And that maybe it should be.

"Well, I'll be happy when this is all over," he admitted, giving a tight laugh.

Dan lifted an eyebrow. He seemed to want to say something and then thought the better of it. "Good thing you have the hotel project to keep you occupied. It's always best to let the women run the show when it comes to the weddings, at least in my experience."

"Any other advice?" Nick asked.

"About the hotel or about your wedding?"

Nick supposed that he was looking for some wisdom about the wedding, something that made these conflicting thoughts banish once and for all. But Dan was still tanned from his honeymoon. His ring was still shiny. And, as he had said, he'd married for the right reasons.

And Nick wasn't so sure that the same could be said for himself.

"The hotel," he said finally. Best to distract himself from the anxiety that was gnawing at his stomach every time he thought of the wedding or glanced at the calendar. "I don't have a lot of support with this project, so the more progress I can report back the better."

"Report back?" Dan asked.

"My father," Nick explained. "Family business."

Dan nodded. "I took over a family business myself. When my father saw that I could handle it on my own, he stepped back. I think he was grateful for the chance to retire, honestly."

Nick could only hope that would be the case for him, but it would take a lot to make Harold believe he was leaving the company in good hands. His father may not agree with his decision to keep the integrity of choice historic properties, but when Nick was finished, he'd be sure that his father would be in no position to question or argue.

There would be no room for doubt.

About anything, he told himself firmly.

*

Chloe pulled Sarah aside the moment that the shop quieted down. It had been a busy morning, which was a good thing, but still, she was rattled. A new business going in down the street could only mean less business for Bayside Brides. Sure, they still captured the market on the retail side; there was no other shop for miles that sold wedding gowns, veils, shoes, and bridesmaid dresses. But the planning side of things...that was where Chloe had always wanted to be. With a push from Melanie, she'd finally gotten there.

And the Addison-Tyler wedding was what could keep her there.

With that in mind, she pulled out her checklist. "Do you know if Chris is open to letting another wedding take place at Crestview?" she asked.

Sarah looked apologetic as she shook her head. "I didn't want to say anything the other night when Lori mentioned it, but he's already going through with the paperwork needed to donate the estate. He had a meeting last week. He was waiting for Hannah's wedding to be over before he made things official."

"So now the estate will be owned by the town," Chloe said. "Are they doing work on it?"

"Oh, quite a bit. It's going to take at least six months to transform it from a residence into a museum. They're planning to open around the holidays, or the New Year…"

Meaning not in time for Lori's wedding. She sighed, thinking that at least Nick would be happy. He seemed determined to hold the wedding at the Oyster Bay Hotel, even if Lori didn't seem quite as thrilled. Still, Chloe would deliver. She had to deliver.

She thanked Sarah and excused herself to fire off a text to Lori, giving her the news.

A reply came quicker than expected: *Can you and Nick meet with the chef at the hotel and narrow down the options?*

She and Nick. Chloe hesitated, her thumbs hovering over the keyboard. Technically, she could send Sarah, who was her assistant, after all. Sarah would be all too thrilled to be asked to step in and help out on this particular wedding.

"Everything okay?" Melanie asked. She had just opened a box of veils, and her arms were full of frothy tulle.

"Just thinking about that business," Chloe admitted.

"Don't worry about something until you know it's worth worrying about," Melanie said. "Have you done any research on them?"

"Not yet," Chloe said. Normally, this was the first thing she would have done. But right now she didn't feel like she could handle any more bad news. She just had to get through the month, and then...then she'd figure out her next step.

"Well, don't let it get you down. You were so happy the other morning. So hopeful." Melanie gave her a hesitant smile, as if she knew that perhaps something hadn't worked out the way Chloe had wished.

"Oh, I just got caught up in the idea of being featured in a big magazine," Chloe said, looking back at her phone. Meet Nick. Could Lori possibly be serious?

"And here I thought you'd met someone," Melanie said, a hint of suggestion in her tone.

Chloe barked out a laugh to cover the racing of her heart. "I don't have time for love. I have a business to run!"

"Love isn't always convenient," Melanie said lightly.

You can say that again.

Chloe just shook her head and went into the back room. She wanted to ask Sarah to meet with Nick, but Lori had hired *her*. Lori was expecting *her*.

As much as it killed her, she had to see it through. And that meant making sure that every detail was up to her personal standards, and that nothing slipped through the cracks. And Sarah, eager as she was, couldn't fully be counted to keep things up to Chloe's standards.

No one could be counted on, Chloe had learned a long time ago. All you had in the world was yourself.

*

Chloe decided to put off contacting Nick until after she had spoken with the chef directly. She went over after work, deciding that her workout would have to wait and excused herself to the kitchen, hating that it was coming up on the dinner rush but seeing no way around it. Josh didn't work in the mornings, the hotel used line cooks for the breakfast service, and Chloe's afternoons this week were mostly booked with dress fittings and a few planning meetings for other brides. Unless she was willing to wait for the weekend, now would have to work.

And she didn't get the impression that Lori would be willing to wait that long for news. Besides, it would make sense to have an abbreviated list of options ready for her to taste this weekend. Less room for criticism. Less time spent on one line item.

Already, Lori had sent her a five-page printed "Wish List" which included everything from a big brass band to men walking on stilts. She seemed to have confused the theme of beach wedding with old-school Atlantic City, and Chloe had spent half the day thinking of ways to politely steer her in a better (and more realistic) direction.

And she'd spent the other half of the day thinking about Nick, and how she should not be thinking about Nick, and how everything about how she had reacted to Nick, from the start, was out of character for her. And that he alone could completely derail her. If she let him.

The kitchen at the hotel was loud and hot and Josh was red in the face, whisking a sauce that Chloe quickly deduced by the rich smell was chocolate. Milk chocolate. Creamy and smooth and oh so sweet smelling. Her mouth watered, but then she remembered her health regimen. Dark chocolate only, for the antioxidants.

That reminded her...For Hannah's wedding, Abby had made the cake, but as the chef at Harper House Inn, and a newlywed, her schedule was tightening, especially now that Bridget had decided to expand their dining hours at the inn.

Out of loyalty, she'd ask Abby if she wanted to throw her hat into the ring, otherwise she'd see how Lori felt about having Josh make the cake.

"Don't tell me, you're here to talk about a wedding." Josh was an old classmate, a few years ahead of her in school, who had gone on to culinary school in Rhode Island and then taken over his father's place in the kitchen of the hotel. He was young, but not inexperienced, but Chloe couldn't be too careful, not when it came to this wedding, not when it came to Lori's expectations.

Chloe waggled her eyebrows. "Not just any wedding."

Josh's face was one of pure shock. "What are you saying? Are...you getting married?"

He made it sounds as if it was the most preposterous thing he'd ever heard of and Chloe frowned. "Jeez, Josh, would that be so unexpected? And no, it's not my wedding."

"Not unexpected. Just...surprising. You never make

any time for romance."

Recently, she couldn't say this was true. But no sense in using that argument as her defense.

"I'm a busy woman," she said with a sigh.

"And I'm a busy man," he replied with a grin. Josh was still dating his high school sweetheart. Chloe knew for a fact that Kasey had been hoping for a ring for some time, but she didn't feel the need to point that out right now. She had more pressing matters to discuss.

"I'm here to discuss a society wedding that will be featured as the main article in the October issue of *Here Comes the Bride* magazine."

Josh let out a low whistle as he tapped the whisk against the side of the bowl. "Here at the hotel?"

Chloe nodded. "The bride is an editor at the magazine and the groom is…"

Handsome. Sweet. Witty. Completely unavailable.

Probably a bit of a jerk.

Except that in her heart she didn't think he was, and that was possibly the worst part of it all.

"Anyway, I'd like to set up a meeting with the groom, this week, if you have time. But before I do, I wanted to give you some time to prepare. These are New Yorkers, so they have high standards. I'm thinking coastal, but refined. After all, this has to be magazine-worthy."

Josh had added a splash of cream and was nodding as he whisked. The smell was heavenly and for a moment Chloe considered breaking her routine and indulging in something before she left. A slice of cake, perhaps.

Flourless.

But then she thought about what happened when she broke her routine. Nope. Best to stick with the tried and true. Even if it was…lonely? Boring? A little of both. At least it was safe.

"I'm hoping to have a meeting this week with the groom, then present some tighter options for the bride when she returns to town this weekend."

Josh pulled an agenda from a pile of papers on a desk in the corner of the kitchen. Chloe could see that the book was stuffed with recipe cards, and each date was filled with shopping lists, menu plans. "I can do tomorrow evening."

Chloe shook her head. Tomorrow was her mother's birthday and she had promised to go over for dinner.

"Thursday then? I can do four in the afternoon or eight in the evening."

Chloe knew that she could make either time work, though she would prefer the afternoon appointment. It would be brief, on business hours, and she'd have an excuse to get back to the shop.

But she would defer to the client. She stifled a sigh at the thought of personal contact with Nick and said, "I'll be in touch once I hear from Mr. Tyler."

"Mr. Tyler?" Josh's eyes grew large. "The man who might be buying the hotel?"

Chloe knew she shouldn't be too disappointed to learn that Nick hadn't exactly been sharing some special secret with her the other day. But she was surprised that word had travelled to the staff.

"Well, then, I guess I have an extra reason to impress him," Josh said. "Between you and me, I hope that Nick Tyler buys the hotel. He has some fresh ideas for it, and we need some changes around town, don't you think?"

Chloe's stomach went all funny when she thought of the event planning shop opening down the street. "I guess I'm different. I like Oyster Bay just as it is. It's…reliable."

Josh just shook his head good-naturedly and went back to his sauce.

"I'll be in touch soon," she promised as she pushed back into the dining room. "Once I hear back from Mr. Tyler."

"Hear back from me about what?" a voice said from behind her, making her jump.

She turned to see Nick, sitting alone at the bar, a beer in one hand, a huge burger in the other.

"Funny, I didn't take you for the burger and beer kind of guy," she said, trying to cover the awkwardness she felt. He was wearing a dress shirt, rolled at the forearms. She stared at them for a moment, thinking of how they'd felt when they caught her fall…

Catching herself, she looked up. He was watching her, an amused glint in his warm, green eyes.

He cocked an eyebrow. "And what kind of guy did you take me for, exactly?"

Single, she thought. Interested. Not that she'd be

revealing any of that.

She shrugged. "More of a fine French wine and a steak type, I suppose."

He laughed and took a sip of his beer before setting it down. "You're mistaking me with Lori. We're quite different people."

Yes, she was beginning to notice that. At the mention of his fiancée, she gave a tight smile and edged away, but then remembered that she still needed to ask him about the menu tasting. She supposed she may as well do it now and save herself the awkwardness of a phone call tomorrow.

"I was just meeting with the chef here. He'll put together some menu ideas and we can narrow down the options for Lori."

His eyes widened and he set down his burger with a grin. "When?"

My, didn't he seem eager. She eyed his burger, then noticed he had ordered an extra side of fries in addition to the heaping mound that was already taking up one side of his plate. Maybe he just liked food, she thought.

After all, he'd given her no real reason to imply that he liked her. He'd been friendly. And she'd read far too into it.

She shook away the tug in her chest. The facts were the facts.

"Thursday?" she asked. "The chef is available at four or eight in the evening. I was thinking that four—"

But Nick said, "Eight works."

"Eight." Chloe nodded slowly. She didn't want to admit that normally she was in for the night by eight, face moisturized, pajamas fresh, a book in hand, or sometimes a movie. Lights out by ten. Up again by five.

But he was a client. And she had no choice.

"I'll see you Thursday then," she said, inching away.

He stopped her, patted the chair beside him. "Have you eaten?"

She had not eaten. She never ate before she worked out, unless it was a bite of a granola bar or a piece of fruit, something for energy. But right now, looking at the expectant grin that lifted the corners of his eyes, and that positively huge, juicy burger that he held in his free hand, her stomach started to rumble with temptation.

A week ago, she would have saddled up next to him, her heart thumping with expectation.

But a week ago, he wasn't her client. A week ago, he was…well, a possibility.

"I'm on my way to gym, actually," she said. She couldn't even remember what day it was right now, but she said, "Pilates class. I should really run." Run, not walk. Eye on the prize and all that.

Something seemed to shadow his eyes as he nodded quietly. Finally, he said, "Sure. I won't keep you. But only because you didn't tell me that you don't eat like this."

She eyed the mound of fries on his place. She most certainly didn't eat like that, but again, he had her thinking of breaking all her rules.

"It's tempting," she said. "But…"

"Pilates. I know." He grinned. "Otherwise I would have taken it personally."

"Nothing personal at all," she said firmly, as she walked away, resisting the urge to look back when she reached the lobby.

Instead she squared her shoulders, walked outside, and kept her eyes firmly in front of her as she headed toward the gym.

It was just as she'd said. Nothing personal at all.

Chapter Seven

The next afternoon after work, Chloe pushed through the doors of Morning Glory, the flower shop just down the street from Bayside Brides. Posy was behind the counter, finishing up with a customer, but she called out to Chloe when she was finished.

"Another big order for me?" She looked nearly as expectant as she did fearful. After all, they'd only just gotten through Hannah's wedding, even though it was starting to feel like half a lifetime ago.

So much could change so quickly. And Chloe of all people knew this best.

She pulled in a breath. She was trying to wrap her head around the planning of Lori and Nick's wedding. Every detail had to be at its best, and the flowers were often the star of the show—aside from the wedding gown, of course, but Lori had that covered. She'd sent the photo over that morning. It was designer, of course, and a well-known one, too. Chloe was relieved to see that it wasn't a ballgown. She rarely thought those worked for a beach wedding. Instead, Lori had gone with something A-line and classic, leaving plenty of options for bridesmaid dresses.

"Not today," Chloe said, "but I'll set up an appointment for this weekend while I'm here. Lori Addison is coming back to town and we'll place our order then."

Posy frowned. Of course she knew all about Lori's wedding. She'd been at Bayside Brides, delivering a bouquet for their center table, when the first email requesting a meeting had arrived.

Again, it was hard to believe that was only last week. Chloe was so full of joy then. So full of…hope.

"Already?" Usually brides had multiple meetings before they actually placed an order. But time wasn't on their side in this case.

"The wedding is the last weekend of the month," Chloe explained. "It was supposed to be in the spring, but then—"

Posy waggled her eyebrows. "A surprise?"

Chloe had to laugh. "No. It's nothing personal. It's because their wedding will be featured in the country weddings issue, and that got moved up."

"Not personal?" Posy repeated. "Shouldn't a wedding

of all things be completely personal?"

Chloe didn't know what to say to that. Technically, weddings should be personal, but more and more she saw other pressures interfere. Still, it was a little strange just how much importance was being placed on the magazine issue and not on the desires of the couple themselves.

But she wouldn't complain. The exposure would be great for business, and right now she needed it more than ever.

Chloe looked around the shop to make sure they were alone and said, "Have you heard about that new business opening soon? The event planning business?"

Posy's eyes went wide. "I passed by it the other day. I think they plan to open soon. September maybe. Why, are you worried?"

Worried sick, Chloe thought. The only way she had succeeded in ending her decades-long nail-biting habit was by now having weekly manicures to keep them off-limits.

Still, she chewed her lip. "Well, it's not good news."

Silence fell while the two women's eyes locked across the counter. Finally, Posy said, "Well, maybe they'll plan birthday parties. Corporate events. Holiday parties, anniversaries…Believe me, there are many occasions other than weddings."

"But why wouldn't they plan weddings?" Chloe said. Her heart rate was picking up. "Oyster Bay is hardly a hot spot for big businesses. And there are only so many people who would want a birthday party planned."

"Summer parties?" Posy tried. "You know how the tourists can be. They rent out those cottages on the shore and want to entertain their friends in style."

"Maybe," Chloe said, but she still didn't feel entirely comfortable. "I suppose it's good for you, though. You're the only florist in town."

But Posy was already shaking her head. "I considered that, so I called and introduced myself. They said they will be using an in-house florist."

"In-house!" Chloe cried. She blinked rapidly, trying to make sense of this. "But the entire point of the Main Street renovation was to drive traffic to local businesses. To support the community."

Posy shrugged. "Guess I'll have to make do with birthday and holiday orders. And, of course, all the brides who come through Bayside Brides."

Chloe felt uneasy. "If they don't try the new place instead." She had been dreading investigating this further, but now she felt she had no choice. She'd see what she could dig up. Maybe they already had a website live.

"So, does two o'clock this Saturday work for the meeting with Lori?" Posy asked, as she flicked through her date book.

Chloe pulled up her calendar on her phone. She had a dress fitting that morning, but she should be able to slip away by two.

"I'll confirm with Lori, but that should be fine," she said as she tapped a text message to Lori. She looked around the room, which usually lifted her spirits with its colorful petals and fragrant aroma. But today her chest felt like a lead ball. "I'm here for a bouquet. Something happy. Something cheerful. It's my mother's birthday," she explained.

Posy nodded. "Favorite color?"

"Purple," Chloe said. "Something…festive."

But even as she said it, she knew that this was a long shot. Still, it was worth the effort. It was always worth a try.

Posy went around the shop and began plucking stems from their canisters, putting together a stunning assortment of roses, freesia, and snapdragons.

"How about this?" she asked, turning breathlessly to Chloe.

Chloe looked at the stunning arrangement in her friend's arms and felt a little more hopeful than she had when she'd come in here. "Beautiful."

Posy grinned and went to the counter to wrap the flowers in brown paper and tie them with twine.

"Have fun," Posy said with a smile, but Chloe's own smile felt wan.

There hadn't been much fun to be had in the Larson household in a very long time.

*

Chloe pulled her car to a stop outside her parents' house and pushed back the sense of dread she had every time she came here. Her parents lived on the outskirts of

town, as far from the shore as one could get without
leaving the town limits. It was a small, two-bedroom
cottage that they had been renting since they'd had to
move out of Chloe's larger childhood home when she
was twelve—old enough to sense the tension in the
house, old enough to think to ask what words like
"repossessed" meant.

"Your father works hard," her mother always said, but
there was a sadness in her eyes that stuck by some point,
and it was that look that kept Chloe from visiting very
often. Work kept her busy. It was an excuse, but it was a
real one.

She needed to work. She needed to be busy. She would
never again feel as helpless as she did that day that they
packed up their belongings into the truck and drove away
from their charming Colonial. She'd sat on the front
stoop, watching as the last of the boxes was loaded into
the truck. The neighbor's cat was always on the prowl,
but it had never come close to her before, no matter how
often she'd tried to call to it. But that day, of all days, the
cat did come and sit by her feet and let her stroke its back
and the little space behind its ears, and it was still there,
watching her, when she climbed into the backseat of her
parents' car and watched her home grow smaller and
smaller in the distance behind them.

For her mother's birthday, she always treated her,
because she knew that her father rarely could and that her
mother would have protested if he had. Her mother liked

to say that she didn't need anything, that she had everything she could ask for, but Chloe knew it was a brave front, just like the smile she kept plastered to her face. Did she think that Chloe didn't notice how she had worn the same red dress to Christmas Eve at Melanie's parents' house for the last six years in a row?

Her mother deserved something pretty, something frivolous. She'd worked two jobs at a time when Chloe's father was out of work, and she never complained.

Chloe opened the door, letting a wave of heat affront her as she stepped onto the gravel driveway. Her father's old navy sedan was in the carport at the end of the driveway, meaning he had either gotten home early for the occasion or he hadn't gone to work today.

Chloe felt a familiar tension creep up as she walked around to the passenger door and pulled out the cake, the flowers, and the signature blue Bayside Brides bag containing her mother's gift. The same old anxiety that bubbled every time she saw one of the red flags: toast for breakfast instead of the cereals she preferred; her mother's overly bright smile that didn't quite meet her eyes; her father hunched over the newspaper when he should be getting ready for work; the way the air seemed to prickle with tension.

Her father's latest job was store manager of a hardware store in Shelter Port, three towns over. He'd had his job for twenty-two months, because yes, Chloe kept track of these things. It prepared her, she'd found. Usually, by about the two- or three-year mark, she could start bracing herself for bad news. Sometimes, though, it hit sooner, like the time that he came home at noon one summer day only four months into his job at the trucking company.

Her father was a good man, she knew. A kind man. He was just down on his luck, she'd come realize. Depressed, one might say. It was a vicious cycle. He'd had a good job once, and then the company had folded, everyone was out of work. And then he couldn't find another of that caliber. He'd started doing odd jobs while he'd looked for something more substantial, but it crushed his spirit, and by the time he got back into the workforce, his confidence was rattled. He was in a lower position than the one he'd left. He didn't see a chance to move up. He was bored and unhappy. And angry. And then he started sleeping late, taking breaks that went on a little too long. And the more jobs he lost, the worse things became.

And when they lost the house…He'd never been the same.

When Chloe was younger, she used to tell her mother that it would be okay, that someday she'd buy them their house back. And she still held onto that dream when she opened Bayside Brides. But now she knew that her father wouldn't want her to buy them a house, just like he probably wouldn't like the gift she had brought for her mother, either. He was too proud, and she accepted that. Still, it was her mother's birthday.

Her mother was in the kitchen, standing over the ancient stovetop, when Chloe approached the screen door. Immediately, she felt discouraged. Her mother shouldn't be cooking in this heat, on her special day. Chloe would have liked to have taken her parents into town, treated them to a dinner at The Lantern, where Chip would toss in a dessert on the house and the wait staff would sing and where they'd be distracted from their troubles for a while, embraced by the community, but she knew how her father would have felt about that.

"Happy birthday!" She forced the cheer into her voice, even though she had the horrible feeling that she could cry.

It was always like this, every time she was here, sometimes worse when she left, and she went home to her empty apartment with its lovely window boxes filled with seasonal flowers and its crisp, white furniture to think about how much her mother looked forward to her visits and how much Chloe was already dreading the next one.

Her mother didn't have time with her work week to come into town or have lunch with her the way Melanie and her mother did. And much as Chloe loved her mother, she hated going to this house, hated the sadness that seemed to linger in the air and stay with her long after she had left.

At the sound of her voice, her mother turned to her and beamed. She was dressed up for the occasion, Chloe noted, in a pink scarf that was at least twenty years old and too warm for this weather, and a touch of lipstick; something that made Chloe's heart sink a little. There were some daisies in a chipped vase on the table near the window.

Chloe opened the screen door and let herself into the house. It was even hotter inside the kitchen than it was outside. She could only hope that there would be a cool breeze this evening, not that she would stay until dark. Her mother went to be bed early, so she would be rested for her early start. She'd been working the breakfast shift at the diner off the highway for the past five years. She liked it, and the tips were good, she said.

Chloe set the cake down on the counter and handed her mother the flowers and gift bag before giving her a peck on the cheek.

"Oh, these are lovely!" Her mother blinked down at the flowers she cradled in her arm. Posy had done a good job of putting something together; but then, she always did.

"Did I hear Chloe?" her father's voice boomed from the back bedroom, and a moment later he appeared, grinning as he leaned in to give her a hug.

"Hey there, Dad." Chloe heard the strain in her voice, felt the hot tears prickle the backs of her eyes and willed them not to spill. Awe, Dad, she thought. She wished so many things for him. Most of all, she just wished that he was happy. That they both were.

"What do we have here?" Her father's smile seemed to slip as he eyed the flowers and gift bag that her mother was still holding.

"It's too much," her mother was saying, but she looked pleased by the flush in her cheeks.

"It's your birthday," Chloe said. "It's never too much."

Her father's jaw set. "Well, I guess we won't be needing those flowers I got you now that Chloe's brought you an entire florist."

Immediately, Chloe regretted bringing the flowers. She looked at the smaller bouquet that was sitting at the center of the table. A cheerful arrangement that paled in comparison with her ostentatious offering.

Maybe her mother was right. Maybe it was too much. But it was something. She had to do something. Because she never could before, all those years, all those birthdays, when she was just a helpless kid.

"Your father knows I love my daisies," her mother said as she reached for a jug and filled it with water. A moment later, the flowers that Chloe had given her were set up on the coffee table in the living room. "Remember how you always used to get me daisies, Chloe? You'd pick them all around town." Her mother laughed.

Chloe remembered now. It was the only gift she could offer up, and it seemed to please her mother to no end.

"Well, why don't you open the gift?" she said, hoping to get away from the comparison of the flowers.

Her mother made a big show of removing the sea foam colored tissue paper and folding it neatly before setting it on the counter, no doubt to be saved and re-used at a future date. She pulled out the white cardboard jewelry box, gasping when she opened it.

"My friend made it," Chloe was quick to say, before she could be accused of it all being "too much." It was true, technically. Beth Sanders had made the necklace, just as she made lots of jewelry for the shop and some private clients, too. Chloe just omitted the part that she had, of course, paid Beth for the work.

"Well, she is quite talented. This is just beautiful. I'll wear it to lunch with Karen this Sunday." It was tradition for Melanie's mother and Chloe's mother to have lunch on their birthday weekends. Just as sisters.

"You'll be the talk of the town," Chloe said. She glanced at the stove, where the water for the pasta was starting to boil over, and shifted past her mother to flick off the burner.

"The table is all set. I'll have everything ready in a few minutes," her mother assured her.

"But it's your birthday," Chloe protested.

Her mother's eyes for once didn't have that flat look. She patted the necklace she'd already hooked around her neck. "And you're my guest of honor."

Could one be a guest in their own home? Chloe supposed it was possible, and this house had never felt like home. Home was a reprieve. A place of your own, where memories were made and laughter was shared.

No. This had never been home. All laughter had stopped by the time they'd moved here.

She took her seat at the table, in between her parents, and let her mother dish her a mound of spaghetti, that she topped with a ladle of tomato sauce. It wasn't part of her diet, but right now, she couldn't worry about that. Her throat felt locked up and she had no appetite, despite skipping lunch because she'd been so busy at the shop today.

"So, how's business?" her mother said.

Chloe twirled the pasta on her fork. "Good. We're still adjusting to all the new changes, and then there's the Main Street renovation project which has brought some new shops to town…" She shoved the pasta into her mouth, grateful for the excuse not to elaborate. She didn't need to dump her worries on her parents. She had a business. So far it was still intact. Her mother was proud of her.

The last thing her mother needed to worry about was her, when she had enough to worry about already.

She swallowed the pasta, wondering if she should reciprocate the question or let it hang, talk about something else, something safe like the weather, or her mother's favorite television program.

"How about you guys?" she asked, holding her breath. She didn't even realize that she was squeezing her napkin in her lap until she felt her nails pressing into her palms.

Her mother gulped her water. "Oh, good, good. I picked up a few more shifts at the diner—"

Uh-oh. Chloe watched her mother carefully. There were lines around her mouth that hadn't been there before. And her roots were showing. She looked tired, and old, Chloe realized sadly. All that stress had aged her.

She should have invited her mother into town, for a spa day or something. But then, she would have just said she didn't have the time, what with her new shifts.

"Your father's taking a break from the hardware store," her mother explained.

Chloe darted a glance in her father's direction, but his eyes were fixed on his plate.

"They brought in new management. It's better for him to find something else," her mother added.

Chloe said nothing, even though she wanted nothing more than to reach out and squeeze her mother's hand, and do the same for her father, too, after she'd given his shoulders a good shaking.

The sadness had returned to her mother's eyes, flattening the light from them. Her mother looked away quickly and then said brightly, "Well, I don't know about everyone else, but I can't wait to try that cake!"

Chloe finally went back to twirling her pasta. "Me too, Mom," she managed, and this time, her smile was just as strained as her mother's.

*

Nick sat in his suite at the Oyster Bay Hotel and looked out the window on the Atlantic. It didn't seem possible that in only a month he would be standing on that very sand, reciting his vows to Lori.

And what were the vows? Had they even discussed that? Was he expected to write something? Knowing

Lori, she'd provide something, or offer to, but that wasn't how he wanted it to be.

He decided to ask her next time they talked. So far, since she'd gone back to New York, they'd played phone tag and exchanged a handful of text messages. It wasn't much different than when they were both in the city, he supposed. She was busy with her life. He was busy with his. They came together for dinners. The nights were short and the mornings started early. On weekends that they both weren't fielding emails from work, they usually had various events to attend, ones that he'd rather skip. But Lori liked to socialize. "You never know," she would say. "We don't want to miss out on any opportunities."

He made a note on his phone to ask about the vows. But not right now. Right now he needed to blow off some of this stress. Get out of this room. Give his eyes a rest from staring at these spreadsheets. Burn off the burger that was settled in his stomach. He'd had one every day since he'd checked in to the hotel. If he kept it up, they'd end up naming it after him.

He could only imagine what Lori would have to say about that.

But, considering she was in New York and he was here, he wouldn't have to.

He changed and went down to the lobby, knowing as he pushed through the doors onto Main Street that he should probably go down to the shore, take a jog on the waterfront. But even the lull of the waves didn't appeal to him tonight. Instead, he thought of the park, with the pond.

And Chloe.

She wouldn't be there. Not now. It was nearly eight at night. She was probably home, wherever home was. Or out with friends.

Or out on a date.

He swallowed hard. That idea shouldn't bother him. It really shouldn't. Not anymore than it should bother him that she seemed to have cooled to him, and that maybe that was his doing. He hadn't exactly been friendly to her the other night at the restaurant, instead chatting with the other women, because it had been…easier that way.

Because it had seemed like the right thing to do. Because he didn't know what else to do.

Telling himself that he could jog where he pleased and that there was little chance of her being at the park in the evening, when her routine seemed to be mornings, before work, he made his way to the edge of town and cranked up his speed where the trail parted on the grass that led to the pond.

He hadn't even rounded the hill when he saw her. Up ahead, on the other side of the pond. Sprinting as if she were running for her life, her arms pumping at her sides, her blond ponytail flying behind her.

He stopped, told himself he should turn around now, head back to town before she'd had a chance to see him. But he still hadn't quite talked himself into that when he saw her lurch forward and stumble to the ground. Even across the distance, he heard the grunt of her fall. She might have gotten the wind knocked out of her. And she wasn't bouncing back up.

His jog turned into a run, and he didn't slow until he reached the spot where she was crouched on the ground, rocking back and forth as she gripped her lower leg.

"You okay?" he asked. Chloe looked up at him sharply, her expression turning from surprise to defiance.

She jutted her chin. "Fine. Fine." But she frowned when she looked back down at the ankle she was holding.

"That was a hard fall," he said. She still wasn't getting up. And until she did, he wasn't going anywhere.

"I lost my footing." Her mouth thinned. She was disappointed in herself, he realized.

"You training for the Olympics?" he joked, hoping to lighten the air. There was tension between them, something strained that he didn't like.

He should have told her that he was engaged. He just hadn't quite been able to believe it himself at that point.

"The Turkey Trot," she said, finally giving him a small smile. "This year, I intend to win."

"Well, that's quite a goal," he said, impressed.

But she just laughed. "Considering that even old Wally Jennings signs up and half the others are walkers, it's actually not. But I want to beat my time from last year. I'm going for a personal best."

He couldn't help but smile. She worked hard, and he liked that in a woman. It was something he'd liked about Lori—once. But lately Lori's hard work had morphed into something else. Something that didn't make him entirely comfortable.

"Do you think you can stand?"

"Of course I can stand," she grumbled, but she was wincing as she pushed herself up from the ground. She brushed the gravel from her palms, limping as she attempted to put weight on her left foot.

"You need to ice that," he said. "How far do you live from here?"

"Not far from where I left you last week," she said. Her cheeks pinked and she looked away. It was the first reference to their interaction before they became wedding planner and client.

Wedding planner and groom.

His mouth went dry at the thought.

"Well, let me help you back," he said. "It's the least I can do."

She looked up at him sharply, and something passed between them. Forgiveness? Maybe just understanding, he thought. He wanted to make things right. He wasn't a jerk. Even if he was beginning to think that's exactly how she saw him.

"Please," he said.

She sighed. Loudly. Tried to walk again and winced. "I'm sure I can shake it off."

"And if you don't?" He raised an eyebrow, and he knew he had her there. "Come on. Let me help you back. I don't bite, you know."

She gave him a look that implied she wasn't so sure, and then, after a very long deliberation muttered, "Okay. Thanks."

He didn't wait for her to change her mind before he reached his arm over her back. She felt warm and small. But she felt something else, too.

She felt right.

Chapter Eight

Her apartment was not far from the park, but this evening, it felt like it was across town. In another town. In another state.

Chloe was all too aware of Nick's presence. Of his hand on her waist. His chest pressed against her back. She tried not to wince as they made their back at an excruciatingly slow pace, her eyes scanning for cars, hoping to see one of her friends pass by so that they might offer her a lift and save her from the misery.

This pleasure.

Because that's sadly what it was, she realized, not long after Nick had first touched her, his grip firm and unwavering, his skin warm and welcome, even on this hot summer night.

It had just been too long since she'd let anyone touch her, that's all it was, or so she told herself as she limped along, her apartment within sight now. As soon as things calmed down at work, she'd address her social life, again. It was always there, on her agenda, it just wasn't her top priority. And how could it be, when there was rent to pay and inventory to order and paychecks to issue, and clients to worry about?

And now she had the new business opening down the street to further take away from the mere idea of a little fun.

So no, she probably wouldn't get to check that box on her agenda this month, and probably not next month either. She'd schedule it for January, she decided. A new year. New possibilities.

But first, she had to get through August.

"My building is just at the top of the hill," she said. Not that she was sure how she would get up there at this rate. Still, he didn't seem to take the hint, so she said, "I can probably take it from here."

He cocked an eyebrow, and she felt something in her chest flutter. She pushed it back into place. Firmly.

He was not an option. He was a client.

"You really expect me to leave you here, at the bottom of this street?"

"I'm sure I can manage," she said. And she would. She'd find a way. She always did.

Remember that, she told herself, thinking of the possibility of competition coming into town. Eye on the prize.

"I'd rather not take the risk," he said. His hand didn't move from its hold on her waist, and despite her growing frustration, Chloe supposed she should be grateful that it didn't. Her ankle was throbbing. How much damage she had done, she couldn't tell.

"I'm not much of a risk taker myself," she admitted. And now was probably not the time to start. She had to be on her game, had to be quick, and swift. She couldn't imagine hobbling around the shop on crutches.

She needed ice. Rest.

And then she needed Nick to go on his merry way so she could forget about him. Forever.

"Really?" He seemed surprised by her admission. "But you own a small business. That's pretty risky."

A sense of familiar panic swelled within her. "I suppose," she said. "But to me, it was less risky than working for someone else, being at their mercy. At least with my own business, I'm in control."

He nodded slowly. "That makes a lot of sense."

It did. Most of the time.

As they approached her apartment, she paused to fumble the keys out of the zip pockets of her shorts. She slipped the key in the lock and a winding flight of stairs met them as they pushed through the door.

"Which floor are you on?" Nick asked.

Chloe almost hated to admit the truth. "Top floor. Three." Oh, why couldn't Amanda be collecting her mail from the vestibule at this moment? Or Trudy. She'd even settle for Trudy. Sure, she wasn't exactly spry, but anything was better than this.

Nick eyed the stairs and then gave her a look that made her unsettled. His eyes roved over her body as a slight smile quirked the corner of his mouth.

"You know, it would be easier if I carried you," he finally said.

"What?" Chloe felt the heat rise in her cheeks. "What? No!"

"The alternative is hopping on one leg," he pointed out. "Three flights."

"I can do it," she said, a defensive note creeping into her tone. After all, she didn't work out twice a day for nothing. It had to pay off at some point. Maybe today was the day she could cash in.

"Just let me carry you," Nick said, his voice low and husky, and even though she knew she shouldn't, even though she knew that if she really tried, she could hop to the third floor, even if her good leg burned and nearly gave out, she could do it, the thought of all this being over, the door closed, Nick gone, sooner than later made her cave.

She nodded. "Okay then. But if I'm too heavy, just say so, I don't want you to pull your back out, or fall—" But before she could finish that thought, he reached under her legs and swooped her up.

He grinned down at her as he swiftly reached the first landing. "You were saying?"

Visions of him missing a step and falling backward down the stairs, with her in tow, seemed to disappear as she gazed into his eyes a fraction longer than she should have. She looked away, embarrassed, and then back again, quickly, relieved to see that he was focused on the stairs again, and that they were nearly at the top.

He didn't set her down again until they were standing outside her door, one of only two doors on the top floor. She pushed her key into the lock, relieved that escape was now just a few (painful) steps away, and turned to give him a brave smile.

"Thank you," she said. "It seems like you're always rescuing me. I'm actually not normally this clumsy."

It was true, she wasn't. But when she'd seen him in the park, she had been so surprised that she'd lost focus, barely sidestepped a duck that had decided to stroll the path around the park rather than go for a swim, and down she'd gone.

He looked down at her ankle, which was slightly suspended in the air thanks to her expert balance. All those yoga classes had at least been put to use.

"Let me help you get some ice. I could take an ice water, too," he added with a gravelly laugh.

She noticed the beads of sweat that had collected at his hairline and felt a twinge of guilt. She supposed the least thing she could do was offer him something cold to drink. He was a client, after all.

She flicked on a light and her hallway came to life. It was a small but comfortable apartment, with a sunny white kitchen attached to a living room with a fireplace, and a large bedroom with an alcove for a sitting area, which she used as a home office.

"It's not exactly a penthouse suite," she explained.

"Are you kidding? This is practically a mansion by Manhattan standards," he said, and she felt better all at once.

She dropped onto the sofa while he went to the kitchen to fetch the ice. She unlaced her shoes. Damn. Her ankle was red and swollen. She could wiggle her toes, and move the joint. But she wouldn't be wearing heels tomorrow. Maybe not even this week.

"Wow!" Nick said from the kitchen. "You must have an amazing cleaning person. I've never seen a refrigerator organized by food group. And the freezer has actual labels on each container."

Chloe gave him a funny look. "Actually, that's all my doing."

He raised an eyebrow, and she held her breath, expecting him to say what everyone did. That she was too uptight, that she needed to relax, have a little fun, would it kill her to break with such a strict routine?

But he just said, "I'm impressed."

There went the flutter again. She pushed it back into place and cleared her throat. He'd walk over with the ice pack. He'd drink his water. And then he'd be on his way.

And she'd…she'd be alone again. Only for the first time she realized that was going to feel lonely. Because for the first time she saw what all the fuss was about, what made her brides get all starry eyed and cry away their carefully applied mascara as the minutes to their ceremony ticked away.

She was giving these brides the happiest day of their lives.

But she wasn't happy, she realized. And she wanted to be.

"Here's an ice pack," he said, coming over with a bag of frozen peas. He gave her sheepish look. "It was the best I could find."

She propped her leg up on the coffee table, next to the bouquet of flowers she'd saved from Hannah's wedding. Her gaze flicked to his, wondering if he noticed.

Unfortunately, it would seem that he had.

"Ah, so you kept them," he said, a little smirk curving the corner of his mouth.

"Well, they're too pretty to throw out," she said hotly. Too expensive, too.

"And here I thought this was you buying into all that…What was that word you used? Superstition?"

"Tradition," she clarified. But it was superstition. Of course it was. Because how could she, of all the single girls at that wedding, possibly be the next to get married?

Still, she thought, as she took the bag of frozen vegetables from Nick and set it on her aching ankle, she couldn't help thinking that it might have been nice, if all those silly little traditions were real, and if there was really a happy ending for her in the cards after all.

*

He should leave. Go back to the hotel. Call Lori. But then, he had called Lori earlier that day, and she'd sent the call to voicemail. He slipped the phone from his pocket. Checked his texts. Still nothing.

It wasn't anything new, but with the wedding quickly approaching he felt the need to connect, push back these doubts, remind himself why he was doing this.

He checked his phone again—nothing.

He glanced at Chloe, then looked back at the options in the fridge, neatly organized. He could only imagine what her closets look liked.

He smiled to himself as he reached for a bottle of wine that was grouped with sparkling water, organic juice, and almond milk, and found two glasses in the exact cabinet that he would have expected to find them, along with other glasses, grouped by size, arranged in straight lines.

"If you weren't already running your own business, I'd have to hire you," he said as he walked back into the living room. He set the wine glasses down on two coasters and said, "I figured you earned it."

Her look was guarded, and for a moment he worried he had overstepped, that perhaps she was still mad at him, or that maybe she didn't like him at all. He was a client. Business was over for the day.

"I suppose you did too," she finally said. "I'm not always so accident prone."

"Oh, you're speaking to a pro here," he said. "Broken arm. Two broken arms, actually, not at the same time. A broken nose. This." Here he pointed to the scar on his chin.

"Where'd you get that from?" she asked.

"Slipping on some rocks at Lori's parents' lake house," he said. "Which I suppose I should be happy they sold years ago, or I suppose that would have been the cover story location rather than Oyster Bay." He gave her a wry smile.

"You guys have been together a long time then," she observed.

"Yes and no. We've known each other all our lives. We grew up together. I've known Lori since she was a scraggly kid with braids and braces. It was sort of always assumed that we'd end up together. Then, when she moved back to Manhattan from California, I guess we just saw each other in a new light. We had some of the same friends. We were both building our careers. It just seemed…perfect, as Lori would say."

"Ah, the dreaded p-word," Chloe said.

She let out a small laugh. It was a nice sound, and, he realized, it wasn't one that he had heard much, at least not in the past week, not since their walk around the pond.

He came over to join her at the edge of the couch. Was it just him, or did she shift away a few inches?

For the best, he told himself.

He eyed the flowers, took a sip of his wine. "I want to apologize," he said, looking at her squarely. "I feel like I upset you, last week, when I came in for the meeting with Lori. I...was caught off guard. And you didn't seem happy to see me."

Chloe looked down for a moment before speaking again. "It's nothing. It's fine. I was just...Well, I didn't know why you didn't tell me you were engaged. You had plenty of time when we walked around the pond."

"It didn't come up," he said, but that wasn't a good enough reason and the look on her face confirmed it. "Honestly, I still couldn't quite believe it myself. I...still don't."

She frowned at him. Deeply. "That you're getting married?"

"The wedding date had just been pushed up. It seemed different when it was months away."

"So you thought you could chat up another girl?" she narrowed her eyes at him, and he realized, that maybe, that's exactly what he had done.

"I'm sorry if it came across that way," he said, and meaning it. "We had a funny connection from the wedding, and, well, I guess you could say that I'm looking to put down some roots here in town, connect with people. I'm sorry if it came across the wrong way."

She shook her head, smiling slightly. "No, no, you didn't really do anything wrong. I was just...surprised too."

Was it him, or did he think he saw a wave of disappointment pass through her eyes? He pulled in a sigh, releasing it slowly. She'd misread the situation for what it was. Only now, the more he got to know her, he wasn't so sure she had misread anything at all.

"I probably should have mentioned something to Lori when we came in for the meeting—"

"Oh, I'm glad you didn't," Chloe said, her eyes large. "I can't imagine she wants to hear that the person she hired to plan her wedding got hit in the head during the bouquet toss. I can assure you that I am usually much more in control of my events."

"You're human," he said. "It's okay to make a mistake or be less than perfect."

"You sound like my cousin. She always says I'm too serious." She took the glass of wine and studied the contents for a moment before taking a sip.

"Have you always been the serious type?" he asked.

She seemed to hesitate before she spoke. "Yes."

"And is there a reason for that?" he prompted.

She gave him a long look. "Isn't there usually a reason for everything?"

"True," he said. All very true. There was a reason, after all, that he'd chosen the Oyster Bay Hotel as the first in his portfolio. There was a reason that he had proposed to Lori.

And there was a reason that he was sitting here, on Chloe's couch. But it was only half to do with the fact that she'd hurt her ankle.

"I didn't have a lot of stability in my house growing up," Chloe said, taking a sip of her wine. "I guess you could say that it made me ambitious from a young age. Student council, clubs, teams. You name it, I was on it."

He saw where this was going. He gave her a rueful look. "More like you were running it or winning at it."

She looked down at her glass, her cheeks turning a little pink. "Well, as I said, I was ambitious." She rearranged the ice on her ankle. Her toenails were painted a pale pink, the same as her fingers. The flowers brought him back to that day, and he smiled now, thinking of the strange turn of events that night. He'd been on the prowl for a drink. In the right place at the right moment.

Only now a part of him wished he hadn't gone to the wedding at all. Hadn't seen her. Hadn't watched Dan and Hannah dance and wonder if he would really look the same when he and Lori got married. If he'd feel as happy.

Nick swallowed hard and looked away. "You grew up here?" When she nodded, he said, "And you chose to stay."

"I like Oyster Bay," Chloe said. "But it's not for everyone."

"It's not for Lori," he said, frowning at her. There was a long pause, and he knew that she wouldn't press him for more. After all, Lori was a big client. But he wanted to open up. Needed to open up, maybe. And Chloe was frank, honest, but she was a good listener.

He supposed it came with the territory.

"Lori's a city girl. I don't think she's thrilled about me buying the Oyster Bay Hotel," he said. "But then, neither is my father."

Chloe frowned. "But I thought you worked for a family business."

"I do," Nick said. "But my father has one vision for the company and I have another. Between you and me, I think he's hoping I'll fail. That he can say he told me so. That he knows best."

"Was it always that way with your dad?"

Nick hadn't stopped to think about that, and he grew silent, a hundred memories filling his mind faster than he could process them. His father was always busy, always working, but he had been more of a family man—once. Back when Nick's mother was still alive, he was happier, lighter, he used to say that he was working for a purpose, to give them a good life, to give Nick something for the future. Then, later, it all became different. The company became Harold's priority. It wasn't the partnership that Nick had been hoping for. Things became strained, and distant. And no matter how much Nick tried to please his father, it never seemed to be enough.

His father, he had realized a long time ago, was unhappy.

"I guess you could say that I don't have the same ambitions as my father. Or Lori, for that matter." He took another sip of his wine. He hadn't admitted that to anyone. Hadn't even wanted to admit it to himself.

Chloe gave him a wry look. "Oh, now, I find that hard to believe. You're buying the Oyster Bay Hotel. You have plans to improve it. You're excited about the project."

He nodded. "I am. I really am. But a historic hotel in a small town in Maine?" He shook his head. "Not the big dreams that my dad has for me. Or the company. He'd rather see me expand to the West Coast."

"And Lori?" she asked after a beat.

He glanced at Chloe. "Lori and I don't always agree."

She arched an eyebrow. "Does anyone?"

"True," he admitted, but there was something nagging him, something that didn't quite sit right, something that told him this was about more than typical wedding planning arguments, more than being caught up in their respective careers.

"You know, my mother grew up in Oyster Bay," Nick said, eager to change the topic to one that filled him with something other than dread.

Chloe looked at him in surprise. "Seriously? What's her name?"

Nick looked down at his hands. His throat felt tight. "Carol Heekin was her name. She passed away when I was twenty."

"I'm sorry," Chloe said, frowning deeply. "I don't think I knew her."

"She only lived here until she was twelve," Nick explained, leaning back on a throw pillow. He almost felt bad for wrinkling it. Everything in the apartment was crisp and tidy. He assumed that the sheets had hospital corners. He stifled a grin. "Then her father moved them to Manhattan. She spent her teenage years there, met my father, and the rest, as they say, is history."

"Is that why you want to buy the Oyster Bay Hotel?"

Nick nodded, thinking of how close it was, that a part of this town, a part of her, could finally be his. "She took me here, once. I was only about eight or nine. My dad was working, so it was just the two of us. We spent two nights at the hotel, walking on the shore, collecting shells, eating out on the terrace." He gave a little smile. "I always remembered that trip. It was the only one like it. Guess you could say that I'm sentimental like that."

"That's sweet," Chloe said.

Sweet, maybe. A little sad too, he thought.

"I always wanted to come back here. To relive that feeling. I even thought about getting a house here. A summer place. A weekend place." Maybe something more than that.

"You're buying the hotel," Chloe pointed out. "That's pretty special."

"Well." Nick firmed his mouth, shifted the pillow behind his back. "Not everyone can understand that."

"Lori's probably just anxious about the wedding. She's a bride." Chloe set her glass on the table and said, "So long as you're both happy."

Both happy. That was just the thing. He wasn't so sure he was happy.

And more and more, he wasn't sure that Lori was either.

"Well, it's late," he said, finishing his glass. "You going to be okay?"

"I think I'll live," she said, and he had to resist the urge to delay the night further. Instead, he carried the empty glasses back into the kitchen. Put the bottle in the fridge, extra careful to set it back where he had found it, and placed the glasses in the dishwasher, which was empty.

"Thanks for having me," he said.

"Thanks for saving me," she replied, grinning.

"Well. Goodnight." He pulled in a breath. Walked to the door. Pulled it open and stepped outside.

He rested his head back against the door for a moment. Truth of the matter was, he wasn't so sure who was saving whom.

Chapter Nine

Beth Sanders stopped by Bayside Brides every Thursday to drop off her newest jewelry creations. They were beautiful, each of them unique, and often sold by the end of the weekend. Chloe suspected that it wouldn't be long before Beth decided to pursue her designs full-time, leaving behind the craft shop, Beads and Bobbles, that she ran with Kelly Myers's assistance.

"How did your mother like her gift?" Beth asked eagerly, as she carefully pulled the boxes containing the bridal sets from a shopping bag.

"She loved it," Chloe said sincerely. "She put it on as soon as she unwrapped it."

"Then why do you look so sad?" Beth asked, looking a bit bewildered herself.

"Do I?" Chloe forced a smile. "Sorry. My ankle is

bothering me. A mild sprain."

"I still don't understand how that happened," Melanie said. She came over to inspect Beth's jewelry, which was now set out on the counter for the women to admire.

Chloe looked down at her feet, which were covered by the most comfortable flats she owned that still looked somewhat dressy. Fortunately, the swelling on her ankle had subsided, and it was just a little sore.

"I told you. I tripped."

Melanie didn't look convinced. "You were on the cheerleading team. You're coordinated. You never trip."

Or slip, Chloe thought. But she'd gone and done both, in the course of a week. All thanks to Nick.

"Believe it or not, I'm not perfect," Chloe said, giving her cousin a wink, and more and more, she wasn't so sure she wanted to be.

Melanie laughed as she held a pair of earrings to her lobes and admired her reflection in the nearest mirror. "I'll remember you said that the next time one of us messes up."

Panic rose in Chloe as she slung her tote over her shoulder. "Nothing happened that I'm unaware of, did it?"

Melanie gave her a strange look as she turned away from the mirror and set the earrings down. "No. And nothing will. Now go have your lunch. And be careful on that sore ankle. Are you sure you don't want me to have Jason take a look?"

Melanie's boyfriend was the town doctor, and the last

thing Chloe needed was to be wasting time fussing over a sore ankle when she had a competitive business to worry about—and a meeting with Nick tonight.

"I'm fine. Really." Still, she was careful as she stepped out onto the sidewalk and made her way across the street to the café. Angie's was a hub of Main Street, and she was eager to see if the new event planning business had posted any advertisements yet.

The bulletin board hung in the vestibule, jammed with posters big and small that seemed to go two layers deep. She clucked her tongue, resisted the urge to discard the expired postings, and tried to find what she was looking for.

It was no use. She glanced from side to side, certain that the coast was clear, before she began removing pushpins and rearranging the papers by topic. Babysitters and pet care services to the left. Tutoring and kids activities just below. Signup sheets for various happenings around town in the bottom right corner.

"What are you doing?"

Chloe jumped and turned to face her friend Leah, her heart rate only slowing down when she realized it wasn't someone who actually minded that she was taking organization liberties.

"Professional habit," she said with a grin, and Leah just shook her head.

Leah was relatively new to Angie's, but she clearly had experience in a kitchen and she'd helped Abby out with

catering Hannah's wedding last month. She was friendly
and talented and she always gave the Bayside girls a free
brownie or cookie when they needed it the most.
"Cheaper than therapy," she liked to remark.

Right now, Chloe felt she could use some of both.

"Can I ask you something?" Chloe asked, knowing
that she was safe to confide in Leah.

Leah's eyes widened a notch. "Sure."

Chloe glanced around again, even though the vestibule
was small and relatively soundproof. The café would be
loud anyway at this hour; even if she was talking at full
volume no one would notice over the din.

"Have you heard anything about that new event
planning company opening down the street?"

Leah shook her head, but she didn't look surprised to
be asked, either. "No. But you might want to ask Dottie
Joyce. She knows everything that goes on around here."

True, very true, but the last thing she needed was for
Dottie to get a whiff of Chloe's insecurities. She could
just imagine the nosy woman spreading gossip about
Bayside Brides feeling threatened by the changes going on
in town. That wouldn't be good for business.

It wouldn't be good for anything.

"I didn't know if they had inquired here about
catering…"

"Oh, that's what you meant." Leah pursed her lips and
leaned in a little closer. "Apparently they have their own
catering staff."

Chloe was acutely aware of her heart dropping into the

pit of her stomach. Doing flowers in house was concerning enough, but catering too? How could Bayside compete with that? A one-stop shop!

"I thought that the entire point of the Main Street renovation project was to…rejuvenate the main strip. To help local businesses and create a bigger tourist appeal."

"Ever heard of cooperative competition?" Leah asked. Even though Chloe had, Leah said, "More businesses drive more shoppers. Maybe it's a good thing that a similar business is opening up nearby. If brides check them out, they might check you out, too."

"Or they might decide not to use us at all," Chloe said. "When they would have before."

"Well, maybe they do. But then maybe they go shopping for their wedding gown and bridesmaid dresses at your shop."

Chloe didn't buy it. Cooperation felt a lot more like competition. And selling wedding dresses was only part of Bayside's business now. She didn't want to go back to just being a retail shop.

"To be honest, I was a little disappointed when I heard that they had their own catering staff," Leah said with a shrug. "I really liked helping out with Hannah's wedding. I was kind of hoping to do more of it."

Chloe tucked that bit of information away. Her first loyalty was of course to Abby Harper, but Abby was increasingly busy at the inn.

"Well, thanks for the update," she said. "And you

know I'd be happy to have your services on a wedding. I'll keep that in mind."

"Thanks!" Leah grinned broadly and then motioned to the door. "Well, I'd better get back in there. Hang in there, Chloe. Bayside Brides is special. No one can take it away."

Chloe chewed her lip and nodded, but her stomach stirred uneasily. No one could take her business away from her. That's what she'd always thought.

But now, for the first time, she wasn't so sure.

*

Nick was the first to arrive in the kitchen of the Oyster Bay Hotel—a large, industrial space that was loud and chaotic. His stomach grumbled from hunger and he eyed the kitchen carefully, taking in the orderly way each cook handled their station, the way Josh, the head chef, oversaw each plate before it made it to the pass.

"You run a good operation here," he told him, once they shook hands.

"I hope you'll approve," Josh said, obviously pleased. "There's a lot of uncertainty around here with the possible change in ownership."

"I have no intention of cutting staff," Nick said firmly, and that was true. This was a fine hotel, with strong reviews and a loyal following of tourists who returned each year for a visit. "I can only hope that if I'm lucky enough to take over that I do it the justice it deserves."

Josh looked visibly relieved as he perked up. "I've

actually worked at a Tyler hotel before," he surprised Nick by saying. "One summer, back in culinary school. Chicago."

"Chicago!" Nick couldn't exactly muster a grin. He knew the hotel. It was one of his father's favorites. From the outside it looked like a beautiful old building, complete with arched windows and paned glass and gothic features. But once inside, all that charm was lost. Nick often felt like he could be anywhere when he entered one of those properties. There was no personality. No sense of warmth or character.

But there were amenities. The latest technology. Clean lines. Harold Tyler was a big fan of clean lines.

"That's the beauty," his father had marveled the first time Nick had seen the Chicago property, which was the first of many like it. "From the outside it looks old, and inside…new!"

Nick thought of the Oyster Bay Hotel, and what his father would do to it if he had his way.

But this was Nick's project. His account. His portfolio. His turn to finally break away from all the expectations he'd lived under, the ones that were supposed to please his father. The ones that he had hoped would just make the old man happy.

"Ah." Josh grinned over his shoulder and Nick turned to see Chloe hobbling up to them. She held up a hand as both men hurried to help her.

"I'm fine, really. Just a little sprain. But a chair would

be nice," she added.

"Come then." Josh hurried to pull out a chair for Chloe. They were seated in the kitchen. "Chef's table," Josh explained. And despite the noise, there was a white tablecloth, a centerpiece of pale pink roses in a silver vase, and an elegantly set table. He unfolded the heavy cloth napkin and set it on his lap.

"Chloe told me that you will want something refined for your wedding," Josh said as he set a variety of small plates on the table. "These are just a few of the passed hors d'oeuvres."

Nick crammed a mini bruschetta into his mouth and eyed the plates, realizing quickly that a tasting was not a full meal. His stomach rumbled. He'd held off on the burger he'd wanted an hour ago, assuming he was saving his appetite for this.

He looked around the kitchen. It was winding down. He could only hope there was a late-night menu, or twenty-four-hour room service. He hadn't thought to check. Now he was certain it would be something he would implement if it wasn't already offered.

Chloe, meanwhile, took a smaller bite. "What do you think?" she asked as he reached for the mini crab cake.

"Delicious," he said. And it was. He could have eaten a platter of them.

She looked pleased, but uncertainty filled her eyes again when she said, "And what about Lori?"

"She'd like all of this," he said with certainty. Clearly, the dinner that Josh oversaw was a big step up from the more casual options offered during the daytime.

"Onto the salad course, then," Josh said. He filled their glasses with white wine and then presented three salads on the table. "Caesar, Caprese, or wedge. If it were my choice, I would choose the Caesar. We make all croutons in house and the parmesan is imported." He gestured to a large wheel sitting on a counter.

Chloe eyed him eagerly. She hadn't touched her wine. "Caesar is classic. I think Lori might find the wedge to be wrong for the occasion, but of course, you know her best."

Nick's stomach rumbled and he cleared his throat to cover the noise, but it was little use. Chloe's eyes sprang open and she quickly pulled her napkin to her mouth to hide her smile.

Josh, mercifully, had disappeared to plate the main course options, which Nick could only hope were larger in portion. He darted his eyes around the kitchen before leaning across the table. "I thought this was going to be a dinner. Like, a meal."

She blinked at him, seeming confused. "It's a tasting," she whispered back. "That means that you try a bunch of things."

"I know," he said. "I just thought that meant, like, a lot of food."

"Full size?" Her eyes widened again and her shoulders started shaking as she clutched a napkin to her mouth. "Sorry, I shouldn't laugh. It's just that—"

And there went his stomach again. A long rumble of thunder that he was powerless to control.

She sputtered on a laugh and reached for the water glass in the center of the table at the same time as him. Their fingers brushed, just enough for him to feel the softness of her skin, before he snatched his hand back.

"Sorry. Wrong glass."

"I'll ask Josh for a bread basket," she said as he chugged back the water, hoping it would do something to calm down whatever was happening.

He cleared all three bites of his salad options. All delicious. But again, only a tease.

His mouth watered when he glanced across the room, at the pass, where a burger was waiting to be served. He could almost taste those truffle fries.

"I have a confession to make," he finally said when the main courses were presented. Three small plates, roughly two good bites of each option. He scraped his fork against the last of the lobster fettuccine and sighed. "I loved all of it. But Lori's the one who is harder to please."

"Why don't we narrow it down to two salads and two entrees? I'd like to present her with as many appetizers as possible. You can never have enough of those," Chloe advised.

"Perhaps when Lori is in town this weekend, you could all stop by the wedding we're holding and see if it meets your expectations." Josh cleared their plates and walked to a nearby desk, which was overflowing with paperwork.

"Wedding?" Chloe frowned. "Who's getting married? Usually I know all the weddings, even if the bride only stops in for a pair of shoes or a tiara."

"Never heard of them," Josh said, looking at a date book. "It's someone from out of town. Big affair. That new event planning company down the road is handling it."

Chloe nodded, but said nothing as she stood and pushed back her seat. She seemed rattled, and more quiet than usual as she thanked Josh and moved toward the kitchen door.

"You okay?" Nick asked once they were in the dining room. It was relatively empty. Service was winding down. Maybe there was a pizza joint in town that was still open. Or Chinese takeout? Anything.

"The ankle…" She grimaced slightly, but something in the furrow of her brow told him there was more to it than that.

"Why don't we get you off your feet for a few minutes, see what's going on in the Garden Terrace?" he suggested, pausing outside the doors.

He sensed the hesitation in her eyes, but she finally shrugged and said, "It would be a great spot for your rehearsal dinner. And I happen to know that they have a late-night menu," she added, barely suppressing a smile.

"Sold," he said. But he realized that he would have been happy to extend the night regardless of the prospect of a hearty meal.

And that was a problem he would need to confront,
and soon.

*

"So," Nick said when they were seated at a small,
round table, the only thing between them a flickering
candle in a pink votive and a small but sweet bouquet of
yellow roses, likely picked from the very bushes that
framed the space. His order was already placed: a burger,
a beer, an extra order of fries that he had offered to share,
though something told Chloe he would be consuming
every last one. "Did you always want to be a wedding
planner?"

"No," Chloe admitted. She smiled up at the waiter as
he set their drinks on the table and reached for her glass
of wine. It was a cool night and she wished she had a
brought a sweater with her. But she wouldn't stay long.
She needed to get home and take notes on the tasting to
present to Lori.

She needed to get away from Nick and these feelings
that wouldn't go away when she was near him.

"I wanted to be my own boss," she said. "And I was
creative. I went to design school but I was mostly
interested in the business courses. It's been a natural
evolution, I suppose. Of course, my cousin Melanie has
pushed me along the way."

"Melanie?"

"She co-owns the store with me," Chloe explained.
"She's the one who encouraged me to take things from a

retail level to full-service."

"You don't look completely convinced by this," he remarked, and Chloe knew she would brush his concern away, put on a brave front. Maybe it was the wine talking, or maybe it was his company, but she couldn't deny the anxiety that was swelling within her any longer.

"We were doing very well as a retail store. Now that we've expanded our services, the stakes are higher and there's more competition."

He gave her a knowing look. "Does this have anything to do with the chef's comment about the wedding this weekend?"

She couldn't deny it, even if she wanted to, and right now she wasn't sure she did. These fears were something she usually kept bottled up inside, only releasing them through exercise, cleaning, or other tried and true methods that had helped her cope over the years. Growing up, she couldn't tell her parents how she felt. It was more than obvious that her mother was already dealing with her own worries. And later she learned that her friends often encouraged her to lighten up, see the bright side. All good advice. If she could only follow it.

Since she couldn't, she eventually learned to keep her feelings to herself. Take action. Work hard.

"It's not ideal to have another event planning company in town," she said.

"It's the nature of business," he replied with a shrug, and the way he said it wasn't dismissive, it was almost…reassuring. "Just because another company offers the same service doesn't mean that they can do what you do. You bring something unique to the table. Figure out what that is, and make it the forefront of your brand."

The forefront of her brand. She'd never thought of it this way before. After all, they offered a retail store, a one-stop shop. That surely set them apart, but maybe, so did something else. The way they interacted with clients. The personal attention. She wasn't sure what it was yet, but she intended to find out.

"I like that," she said, smiling. "Thank you. You've…made me feel a lot better." He seemed to have a knack for that, she thought. Lending a helping hand, just when she needed it the most.

"I wish I could take my own advice," he said with a laugh. "Sometimes I have doubts, too."

"About the business?" she asked, thinking what he had told her about his father.

"About the wedding, really." He frowned at her.

Chloe did her best to keep her expression neutral. This was prickly territory in any situation, and she wasn't sure that she was the best person to be having this conversation, and certainly not the most objective.

"I'm still trying to wrap my head around getting married in a few weeks. Lori…she just sort of sprang this on me."

"You mean you didn't decide to move up the date together?" Chloe stared at him. She hadn't even connected that part. Of course, this was all sudden to her, as the event planner. But to Nick too?

"It didn't seem like that part was open to negotiation," Nick replied. His mouth thinned.

Chloe took her time configuring a response, even though what she wanted to say was that all of this was a red flag, and a big one. But Lori wasn't here to defend herself, and this was not Chloe's relationship to comment on. Nick and Lori had history. Deep history, from what she had learned.

And she knew firsthand just how influential the past could be.

"If you have concerns, I'm sure Lori would want to know," Chloe said.

"Maybe, but we are holding the event here, at the hotel. Perhaps we've both compromised a little."

He was a nice guy. A good guy. Chloe just hoped that Lori knew it.

"It's your wedding day, too. It should be special for both of you."

He took a sip of his drink and set it down. "I have a feeling that you didn't get into wedding planning only because you wanted to run your own business. There are many options, after all."

She smiled. He had her there. "I suppose I like the idea of the guarantee of at least one good day."

He squinted at her. "One good day?"

"Well, think about it. You never know what the future

will bring. You can't even count on tomorrow. All you really have is today, and making the most of it."

He looked at her somberly and she knew that he was thinking of his mother.

"Marriage is a long road. Life is full of bumps. But a wedding day…it's the happiest day of someone's life. One day that someone can cherish and look back on…well, then I want some part in creating that."

"I don't know whether to call you a romantic or a cynic," he said with a laugh, but he was looking at her strangely, too closely, and she shrugged to lessen the moment.

"Maybe a little of both. When you've been in this business for as long as I have, you've seen it all." And she had. Couples who had overcome break-ups to be reunited at long last. Couples who probably shouldn't be getting married and yet still did, because they didn't know how to turn back once everything was set in motion.

She eyed Nick and took a slow sip of her wine.

"So what's your prognosis on my situation?"

She blinked at him, her mouth dry for a moment while she tried to pull her mind away from the warning signs that were flashing at full volume.

She was biased, she told herself. Because Nick was…wonderful. And unavailable. And sure, maybe he did deserve someone better than Lori, but that didn't mean she should be the one to have him.

"You seem like a well-suited match."

He went quiet for a moment. "Maybe."

She looked at him sharply. "Wedding jitters are completely normal," she said, even though she wasn't so sure that this was the correct diagnosis. She'd come across plenty of brides with nerves leading up to the wedding, and since shifting into wedding planning, she'd seen her share of tie-loosening grooms, too.

But there was a distance between Lori and Nick that she hadn't seen before.

But then, there was usually much more to anyone than was obvious on the surface.

Nick raised his eyebrows, but before he could reply, his phone began to vibrate on the table.

"Oh, it's from Lori." His brow pinched as he read the text and then set the phone back on the table. "It looks like she won't be able to make it to Oyster Bay this weekend after all. Some work trip to California instead."

Chloe tried not to let the panic show on her face. "But the arrangements. Flowers need to be ordered. The invitations!"

Lori had sent the guest list and addresses, but they still had to agree upon the envelope style and font color. She made a mental note to email her some options first thing in the morning.

Nick gave her a funny look. "Guess it's just you and me."

You and me. Invitations and flower arrangements and rush orders aside, Chloe liked the sound of that. And she shouldn't.

Chapter Ten

"You've been strangely quiet all day," Melanie observed when the last of the appointments finally left. "You're not getting worried about Lori's wedding, are you? Although I have to say that it is very strange that she didn't come to town this weekend."

"She had to fly out to California for work," Chloe explained as she pushed a set of satin stilettos back into their box and covered them with tissue paper, careful not to rip it. "She sent me her thoughts on the invitations and some flower ideas, though. Luckily Posy works quickly. And so does Jessica." With any luck, the invitations could go to the printer first thing Monday, for a rush order.

The flowers were more worrisome, especially if Lori didn't select something that Posy kept in stock. And at the rate this was going, Chloe was bracing herself for more complications. She was pushing hard for peonies and roses. They were timeless, they fit the theme of a country wedding, and they'd look beautiful against the blush bridesmaid gowns.

"And you have Nick in town," Melanie pointed out.

There was a long silence. Normally they might have a joke about this; after all, grooms were rarely much help when it came to things like cake styles or centerpieces. But this was no laughing matter.

"How did the menu tasting go the other night?" Melanie asked as she came over to straighten the jewelry in the case.

"Fine. Easy. He isn't hard to please." It was the truth. Nick was extremely easy to spend time with. Too easy, she was finding.

Melanie gave her an appraising look. "You know what I think?"

Chloe's face heated as she stared at her cousin.

"I think that you're worried about the new business going in down the street."

Oh. That. Chloe hadn't even realized she had been holding her breath until it escaped her.

"They have in-house catering and a florist," she said.

"And we have a beautiful storefront full of sparkly things," Melanie pointed out, waving her arms around the store. "People like sparkling things."

Chloe gave a small smile. "I see your point."

"And we offer custom dresses. We're more a one-stop

shop. We…specialize."

"But they're big," Chloe said.

"And we're growing!" Melanie said.

Chloe shoved the last shoebox back onto the shelf. She wished she could have the confidence that Melanie possessed, but life just felt too uncertain. And frankly, too often she felt alone.

Except recently, she thought. It felt good to share her thoughts with Nick. And even better to take his practical advice.

"Well, speak of the devil," Melanie murmured.

The wedding bells jangled, signaling that the door was opening, and Chloe turned to see Nick standing in the frame, looking about as out of place as every other man who dared to cross the threshold.

"Nick." She frowned in concern as she carefully moved around the jewelry case to meet him. "Did we have a meeting?"

She hadn't checked her phone since lunch. It was entirely possible that Lori had sent another message.

Nick glanced at Melanie, who gave him an amused smile and then disappeared into the back room, leaving them alone in the storefront. Chloe was painfully aware of the way his eyes crinkled at the corners when he leaned back on his heels and grinned at her.

"What do you have going on tonight?"

She startled, tried to think fast just as much as she was trying to get where he was going with this question. What did she have going on tonight? It was Saturday, not that this mattered. She had her workout, now that her ankle was feeling better. She had days of lost training to make up for. She had the guest list that Lori had sent over to consider and cake options to pull together and…What did he even mean? What did he even want?

"Because I'm thinking, if you're not busy, that you should come with me to the hotel."

"To the hotel," she repeated. She was fairly certain that all the blood had drawn from her face.

"There's a wedding going on tonight, as I am sure you are aware, and I am in need of…a plus one?" His eyebrow crooked. "Or should I say, a partner in crime?"

"The wedding Josh mentioned?" She stared at him, aghast.

He tossed her a boyish grin. "The very one. What do you say?"

"But we're not invited!" she exclaimed. He couldn't be serious, but looking at the way his eyes shone, she was fairly certain that he was. A thrill boiled up inside her. A chance to scope out the competition, in action. A chance to take back the control, that was rapidly slipping away.

And a chance to do something other than go for another boring jog. Eat another boring meal. Watch another boring television show. Alone.

"So?" His eyebrows waggled. "You have a wedding to scope out, and I have due diligence to conduct."

For a moment, she thought he was referring to his upcoming wedding, but then he said, "I need to know the hotel I'm buying can handle an event, don't I? What do you say? Meet me at six thirty? The reception should be in full swing by then."

She thought fast. Another workout skipped. A wedding basically crashed. And a man who was entirely unavailable leading her astray.

It was reckless. It was brilliant. It was entirely unlike her.

And for the first time in forever, she didn't care.

"See you then," she said, biting her lip to hide its smile.

*

At six twenty-five, Chloe arrived at the lobby of the Oyster Bay Hotel in a pale pink satin sheath, her eyes darting from side to side. By the way her heart was pounding, she was fairly certain that she didn't need to worry about missing that workout after all, and she had to admit that this was considerably more exciting than another lap around the duck pond, or another mile on the treadmill.

The elevator doors slid open and Nick emerged, in a navy suit and pink tie, looking every bit the part of the sleek hotelier that he was, that was until he got a little closer and she saw the gleam in his eye.

"We match," she observed, motioning to his tie and her dress.

"Somehow I'm not surprised," he said, holding her gaze until she had to look away.

"My ankle's feeling better," she said lamely, motioning

to her feet. She glanced around the lobby, feeling nervous and out of place.

Finally, Nick spoke.

"Are we really going to do this?" he asked in a stage whisper.

She felt her eyes bulge. "But you're the one who suggested it!" She looked around again, and lowered her voice as she leaned in. "You made this seem like a good idea."

"I know," he said, grinning. "But it's not like I'm an expert at this."

"You mean you've never crashed a wedding?" she asked.

He looked at her as if she were half-crazy. And maybe she was. He was certainly bringing out a side of her that she didn't recognize.

"Of course not," he said. "Have you?"

"God, no!" What kind of girl did he think she was? A girl who crashed weddings? A girl who fell for a client? A girl who fell for an engaged man, she thought, miserably.

"Well, I didn't come this far to turn back now," she decided, and she hadn't, she realized. Not with Bayside Brides. Not with her own dreams and hopes. She was dressed. Hair done. Makeup applied. It would take too long to undo all this and then get to the gym. And she didn't want to spend her evening that way, she thought, looking Nick up and down.

But she should. For many reasons.

"Okay then," he said, crooking his elbow in her direction. "Shall we do this?"

She hesitated before linking her arm through his, trying to fight the heat that flared at his proximity, and focused on the party that was already underway on the terrace, at the far end of the lobby.

"So, I know why I'm crashing this wedding," she said. "But what's your excuse, truly?"

"It's like I told you. If I'm buying this hotel, I have a reason to see how things are done, and a big event is a test of the management that's currently in place."

"True," she said, but she sensed something else was driving this impulse.

"And I guess I saw it as sneak peek. Of my own wedding," he said, glancing down at her.

There was something troubled in his eyes, but she nodded. "Sensible. Extreme, but sensible." Of course, she could only hope that the wedding she planned would top whatever they were about to walk into.

Nerves fluttered in her stomach. There was music. A band. She still had to book the music. It was something she had planned to do this weekend, but without Lori's input, that left her timeline tighter than ever.

"I'm not so sure this was a good idea," Chloe said as they reached the French doors that led to the reception. "What if someone recognizes me?"

"You heard what Josh said. It's a destination wedding. No one here knows you. Or me."

"The hotel staff?" she pointed out.

"They won't question me," Nick said. "Stay by my side. Tonight, you're my plus one. Besides, our purpose here is purely professional. Surely they can't argue with that."

Purely professional. Something to keep in mind, she told herself as they stepped outside, where the chatter of guests seemed to swallow them in. Chloe let her eyes roam, taking in the details. White flowers, all roses, and while elegant, somewhat unoriginal. There were white tablecloths on the round tables, and small votives circling each centerpiece. All eyes were on the bride and groom, who were cutting a cake as a photographer snapped his camera.

"What do you think?" Nick lowered his head to whisper in her ear, sending a shiver down her spine despite the warm evening.

"Pretty," she said slowly.

"But?" He glanced down at her.

She almost resented that he could sense her hesitation. Few others could pick up on her subtleties.

"But I think your wedding will be better. I mean, I know it will be. For starters, there needs to be some color. And lighting. And ambience. You can't rely on the backdrop of the hotel and the ocean. You want to create a mood."

"Sounds like these event planners missed the mark then," Nick said with a little grin.

"It's a beautiful wedding. It's just...not what I would

do." And there it was, she supposed. Exactly what he'd told her last night. She had to be herself. Do what only she could do.

And let people decide if that was enough.

And that was where she struggled. After all, you couldn't control what other people did with their lives, could you? If you could, then she knew she would have made things much different for her parents, a long time ago.

"So you're more comfortable with what you're offering than what you think these people at the new company could offer?"

Chloe gave a little smile. He had a point, and a good one. "Yes. I suppose that's exactly what I'm saying."

"Then trust yourself," he said. "Some of it's in the gut. Some of it's instinct. Some of it is just pure passion."

"You speak from experience," she said.

"I do. And it's why I am so excited to have this hotel be the first in my portfolio," he said.

Nick pulled her to a stop near the edge of the dance floor, where they had a full view of the reception. They watched, quietly, from a distance, Chloe whispering to him what she would have done differently. More color. More personal touches. The bar should have been moved to the opposite end of the terrace where it wouldn't partially block the view.

"What would your wedding be like?" he surprised her by asking.

She felt her cheeks flush and she looked away.

Watched the bride gingerly cut the cake, smiling for the photographer, anxiety in her eyes every time the skirt of her dress skimmed the table.

"Oh, I'm too busy planning other people's wedding to worry about my own," she said.

"Come on," he said. "You mean to tell me that you're a wedding planner who has never thought about your own wedding?"

"That's right." She dared to look at him, but when she locked his eyes her heart fluttered dangerously fast, and she had to look away. She stared at the tables, noticing that there were no place cards. She managed not to tsk under her breath.

"Uh-uh. I don't believe you," Nick said, elbowing her lightly.

Now Chloe stared him. "Why is it so hard to believe?"

"Because you clearly pursued a career that you love. Because you're clearly passionate about it. That didn't come about randomly."

She pulled in a breath. He had her there.

"No. It didn't," she said sadly.

"Then go on," he urged. "What's your dream wedding?"

Chloe thought about the wedding that she had imagined, ever since she was a little girl and she stumbled upon her parents' album. The photos were old, faded, but her mom and dad had never looked happier. Her mother wore a white dress with flowers on it, and her father wore a white tuxedo. Melanie's mother had been the maid of honor, in a pale blue chiffon dress, her hair half pulled back with flowers. Chloe had never seen her mother so radiant. Nothing could spark that in her again. Not the flowers she'd picked for her kitchen table, not the cards she made on holidays. And all Chloe could think was that if her mother could be this happy on her wedding day, then Chloe could too.

"The funny thing is that I always wanted to get married here," she admitted.

"Here?" Now he looked at her sharply. "At the hotel?"

"When I was little, yes. It seemed like the most beautiful building in all of Oyster Bay. It still does," she said, a little wistfully. She'd long since given up her dreams of a wedding. And she didn't necessarily believe they led to happy endings either. Her parents were a shining example of that.

"Why here?" he asked, looking at her gently.

She pulled in a breath. She wasn't sure she wanted to talk about this. It was something she didn't dwell on. Something she didn't hold on to, even if a part of her never wanted to let it go.

"Well, there was a birthday I had here, when I was about eleven. My parents took me here for high tea. We got all dressed up, all three of us. My dad said he had a surprise for me. We came to the hotel, and we sat in the Rose Terrace, and I just remember feeling like…life was beautiful. The flowers were blooming and there was a harpist in the corner and then there were all these little cakes and sandwiches. I even remember the pattern of the china," she admitted. "It was white with little strawberries around the edge. I don't even know if they still have that."

"It must have been a really special birthday," Nick said.

"The most special," Chloe said, nodding. And the last of its kind. She glanced at him, shrugging. "After that, my dad lost his job. And things, well, they changed." They locked eyes for a moment, and without saying anything, his hand brushed up against hers, and gave it one quick, tight squeeze.

"Lovely wedding, isn't it?" an elderly man alarmed her by saying, and she jerked her hand away.

Chloe glanced down at him and then up at Nick, who gave a tight smile and said, "Just lovely." He turned his body away from the man, as if that was that, but the man, it seemed, had other ideas.

"Are you a friend of the bride or the groom?"

Chloe and Nick exchanged a look of alarm, each searching the other's face for a clue, a hidden message, a direction that they should take.

"Oh, the bride. An old college friend," Chloe said. She could feel her cheeks burn at the lie, and she wished she had some of that cold champagne right about now, just to cool herself down, even if she wouldn't be able to live with such a thing because she knew what the headcount was on a wedding like this, and it was one thing to crash and observe, and another to poach.

"Oh? Funny. I don't detect a British accent in you." The man frowned at her, deeply, and Nick's eyes flashed.

"Study abroad program," he said quickly. Then, as one song ended and the next began, he wasted no time in saying, "Oh, honey. My favorite." He gave an apologetic smile at the man. "You don't mind if we excuse ourselves?"

"Of course not," the man said gruffly. "It's nice to see young people enjoying themselves. Enjoy. Give your girl a good time."

His girl. Chloe was still processing those words when Nick casually sipped his hand into hers, leading her out onto the dance floor.

"We should get out of here," Chloe said. "I've seen enough."

Nick just cocked an eyebrow as he looked down at her. "But this is my favorite song."

She frowned. She'd assumed that he had just made that part up on his feet. And they should go. For many, many reasons, they should march straight back into the lobby, bid each other good night, and part ways.

But his hand was warm and smooth and determined as he led her to the center of the dance floor, lifted her arm over her head for a single pirouette, and expertly pulled her into his arms.

"You're good at this," she said, as he swayed her to the music. She supposed there would be no need to suggest dance lessons to Lori and Nick. Clearly, they'd already taken them.

"I used to dance with my mom," he surprised her by saying.

She looked at him. Amused. "Really?"

"My dad was always busy working, and the country club near our house had these dinner dances in the summer. She taught me to dance. She said I was her partner. Her little man." He grinned, but there was sadness in his eyes.

"Well, she taught you well," Chloe said, hoping that he wasn't going to try any attention-seeking moves and dip her or something. The last thing she needed was for speculation about their presence to arise.

But he held her close, swayed to the music, and for the first time since he'd pulled her onto the floor, she listened to the words.

"Is this really your favorite song?" she asked. It was old. Frank Sinatra. Not one of the usual songs you heard at weddings, either.

"What can I say? I'm an old soul," he said.

She looked up and their eyes met, and for one warm and tingly moment, it was as if the entire world stopped. The music. The party. The people around them. All gone. And all she saw was him. The warm and funny and friendly Nick. His eyes were on hers, so intense that she wasn't sure if they would ever pull away, and she wasn't even sure that she wanted them to. She knew that look. She'd seen it a few times, but still, never like this. It was the look of a man who was going to kiss her.

And she wanted him to. Just as badly as she shouldn't.

From somewhere behind them, a cry went out, and just like that the spell was broken. She pulled back as the music stopped, her cheeks flushed, her hands shaky. Nick stayed put, staring at her.

She looked around. Gathered her bearings. The women were all lined up, not far from them. The bride was going to toss her bouquet.

"You going to try to catch it?" he asked, giving her that grin that made her heart roll over. The same grin he'd given her that first night they'd met. On a night just like this.

She shook her head sadly. She'd caught enough bouquets for one lifetime. And she now knew that even though the man she was falling for was about to stand at the end of the aisle, she would never be the one meeting him there.

"I should probably get going," she forced herself to say. She jutted her chin to the older man who was still watching them, smiling ear to ear. "That was a close call back there."

Nick nodded, but stopped her before she could turn to go.

"Dan invited me to his birthday bash tomorrow night," he said. "Will you be there?"

"Of course. Hannah's a really good friend," Chloe said. The party had been on her calendar for a month. Dan's gift was already purchased and wrapped.

"So I'll see you there then," Nick said, giving her a hopeful look.

And just like that, all good intentions drifted away and she found herself looking far too forward until the next time they would meet.

Chapter Eleven

Chloe was grateful for the busy day at Bayside Brides, not only because it made her less anxious about the new business opening up down the street, but also because it kept her mind from wandering to thoughts of Nick, who she'd be seeing again in—she checked her watch—less than two hours.

Her heart picked up speed as she boxed up a custom order veil, this one with four layers of tulle. "I like the whole poufy bride look," the customer had admitted sheepishly that very first time she'd come into their shop nearly a year ago.

Now that wedding was two weeks away. Chloe wasn't planning it; all that had happened before Bayside Brides had expanded their services, but still, she felt like she had a part in it.

"Well, I can say with confidence that you will make the pouffiest bride we have ever seen," Chloe said now, grinning. Of course, she did have to wonder how the bride would fit into the back of the classic Rolls Royce they had apparently rented to take them to the church. And there was also the matter of fitting through a standard door. There were ten layers of tulle on the skirt of that dress. It was like a confection. Like a beautiful cloud of cotton candy.

The bride twirled in front of the three-way-mirror once more, nearly taking out the floral arrangement that was resting on a pedestal table. Chloe reached for the vase as it teetered and caught Sarah's wide-eyed stare from across the room.

"I'm not ready to take it off just yet," the bride said, and Chloe resisted the urge to tap on the face of her watch. Technically the store was closing in ten minutes, but she never left directly after locking up. There was still more work to be done. Alterations to make and orders to place and cleaning to do, and that only covered the retail end of things. On days like this, when the shop itself kept her so busy, she usually reserved her planning work for after hours.

But not tonight, she thought.

She looked up to see Melanie, back from one of her custom dress design meetings.

Good. With Melanie back things would move much quicker. With any luck she'd have time to run home and change into something more comfortable before heading over to Dan's house.

Make that Dan and Hannah's house.

"It's such a shame to think that you only get to wear it once," the bride was saying, and all three Bayside women clucked their tongues in agreement. This wasn't the first time they'd heard this complaint, after all. Not that any of them, all still yet to be married, could comment personally.

"Who said you only get to wear it once?" Sarah suddenly said, and Chloe glanced at her, not sure where she was going with this. "When I finally get a wedding dress of my own, you'll be seeing me in that thing for years."

The bride laughed, and Chloe did too. It was no joke that Sarah had always been a little wedding crazy. More than once, Chloe had discovered her standing in the dress closet holding up gowns to her chest in front of the mirror, sometimes not even noticing that anyone was watching until Chloe cleared her throat. Loudly.

"I'll vacuum in it. I'll watch movies in it. I may even garden in it," Sarah continued, and despite everyone's laughter, Chloe knew that this was true. That one day she would knock on Sarah's door and find her standing in her wedding gown.

It was the reason she had hired her. It was also the reason she probably shouldn't fear that company going in down the street, she told herself, thinking of what Nick had said last night.

She had to trust herself. And part of trusting herself was trusting her team.

"Well, now I suppose I don't feel so bad taking it off," the bride said, heading toward the dressing room. Sarah tossed Chloe a wink before following. It would take at least one person to get the bride out of that dress. And possibly two to get it all sealed into its bag again.

"It's hard to believe that the next time I wear that dress I'll be walking down the aisle!" the bride was beaming when she emerged from the dressing room a few minutes later. Melanie went to help Sarah carry the dress to the dress closet where it would be stored until the bride chose to pick it up. Couldn't risk having the groom seeing it early, after all. And that was one superstition that Chloe agreed with. You could never be too careful, after all.

"I hope it's the day you dreamed of," Chloe said as she handed over the box containing the veil.

The bride flushed, and her eyes were bright and shiny. "It will be. Every little girl deserves to grow up and have one special day."

It was a sentiment heard often, from nearly every bride that came into the store. But not, Chloe thought, from Lori. She glanced down at her phone, seeing if Lori had replied with opinions on the invitation samples she had sent her. She hoped to get the order in to Jessica Paulson, who did custom invitations, early this week. As it was, she would be asking for a rush order.

But her phone had been silent all day. She supposed that even on a Sunday, Lori's meetings in California were currently taking precedence over the wedding.

Well, none of her business, she told herself firmly. Besides, if Lori wasn't worried about things, then she supposed that she was allowed to have a night off from worrying about it too.

She had a party to get to. And yet again, she was rather looking forward to giving up her routine for something new.

*

Nick was just about to head over to the address Dan had texted him when there was a knock on his hotel room door. He frowned, wondering if the housekeeping crew was dropping something off, and walked to the door.

"Lori!"

"You don't look very happy to see me," she said, grazing his cheek with a kiss as she brushed past him into the room. A bellhop was behind her, with three suitcases.

"Just…surprised," he said, only that wasn't completely true, he realized. He'd been looking forward to tonight. A simple barbeque at Dan's house. A few locals he was getting to know gathered for beer and burgers. Where would Lori fit into the mix? Would she even want to go?

Then he remembered that Lori was of course friends with Hannah. Maybe that was why she had come back to town early.

"Are you here for Dan's birthday?" he asked.

"Dan?" Lori stared at him in confusion from the bed, where she was perched. "Oh. You mean Hannah's husband? No. Why?"

"There's a party tonight. At their house. I was just about to leave."

"A party?" She pouted. "But I haven't seen you all week."

He wanted to ask whose fault that was, because after all, she was supposed to have been in town this weekend, but that wouldn't be fair, he knew. She was overseeing a story. And it wasn't like he was back in Manhattan much these days.

"Hannah will be there," he said.

Her brow knitted, just for a moment, as if she were thinking about something. "Of course. I've been wanting to catch up with her anyway."

"I can wait," he said. "If you need to change."

She looked down at the dress she was wearing. Silk. Black. Formal, even for air travel.

"It's a party. I think this should be fine," she said.

Nick slipped the room key into his back pocket and stifled a knowing grin. There was no point in arguing with Lori, but he had a bad feeling that by the end of the night they'd be arguing regardless.

※

Nick was the first person Chloe saw when she walked

around the back of Dan and Hannah's house to the yard that was set up with lawn chairs and folding tables. The grill on the deck was already smoking and she saw the Harper sisters gathered at the table near it, sipping margaritas.

Nick was sitting in the shade, on a splintered wood chair, sipping a beer, his eyes covered by sunglasses, chatting with Dan.

"Happy birthday," Chloe told Dan, leaning in to give him a kiss on the cheek. She handed him a bag containing wine, chips, and fresh guacamole from the Corner Market, and a smaller bag containing his gift (a leather frame), and then glanced at Nick, feeling suddenly awkward and nervous about how to best greet him, and decided on a smile. "How are you?"

"Hot," Nick said with a booming laugh.

"I'll bring this into the kitchen," Dan said. He glanced at Chloe as he stood up. "What can I get you while I'm there? Margarita? Wine?"

"Wine sounds good," Chloe replied. Anything stronger would just go to her head, and she needed to keep things clear today. Last night had been a close call, and one that she couldn't afford to make again.

"Be right back," Dan said as he walked away.

"Take your time," Nick replied, grinning as he slid his eyes to Chloe.

She stiffened, not sure if she should read into his comment. But he patted Dan's chair and said, "Now that's how you grab one of the few remaining spots in the shade."

Aw, now, why'd he have to go and do that? Because he was nice, she told herself. And charming. And thoughtful. And a dozen other attributes that made him impossible to resist.

Her heart tugged at the way his grin spread all the way up his face to the corners of his eyes.

She'd just cool off. For a few minutes.

"Thank you," she said, sliding into it. It was a hot day, not atypical for August, and enough to make her yearn for the refreshing months of fall, just around the corner now.

She fought back a twist of disappointment when she thought of what this fall would bring, though. Nick would be married. And she would still be here. In Oyster Bay. Planning the happiest day of everyone's life. Except her own.

"I didn't mean to interrupt anything with you and Dan," she said.

"Just shop talk," he said. "I probably shouldn't be bothering him with work stuff on his day off."

"I'm sure he doesn't mind," Chloe replied.

"It seems to be a pattern of mine lately," Nick said, glancing at her. "Thanks for hanging out with me last night."

Hanging out. Was that how he described it? She resented that he could sum it up so neatly, when she was at a loss for how to explain the time she spent with him.

"I don't mind either," she replied softly. She met his eye and then flicked it away, toward the deck, just in time to see a woman stepping out of the sliding glass door.

She did a double take, the moment with Nick forgotten.

It was Lori. She was in her signature head-to-toe black, in an effortlessly chic sundress, her hair pulled off her face, which was covered by her signature sunglasses.

Chloe quickly stood up as Lori and Dan approached.

"Lori. You're here!" That didn't come out right. And her voice, it was too high, like she was nervous or uncomfortable. And the truth of the matter was that she was both.

But she was something else too. She was disappointed.

She took the drink from Dan and resisted the urge to gulp half it back.

Lori was wearing a dress that tied at the waist and fell at her knees. And even though it was sleeveless, she looked about as uncomfortable wearing it as she did in the stiletto sandals that laced up her ankle.

"I thought this was supposed to be a party," she said, as soon as Dan had walked away to greet more guests. She gingerly inspected the seat beside Nick, brushed at it with her hand, and still decided not to sit down.

Chloe looked around the yard, at the women in tee-shirts and shorts, or, like her, cotton sundresses which now felt a little plain, and gave a shrug. "It's a party. Just…a casual one."

"Everything in this town is casual," she remarked.

"It's a beach town," Nick replied flatly, and Chloe stayed silent, noting the obvious tension that was growing between them.

Feeling the need to finally interfere, she mustered up a smile and said, "Well, your wedding won't be casual. Did you see the invitation samples I texted you? Although, now that you're back, we can go over everything in person. Does tomorrow morning work?"

Slow down, she scolded herself. She was talking too fast, trying to keep up with her mind, which felt like it was spinning, and her heart, which was pounding so hard she could hear it in her ears.

Lori was back. She and Nick were getting married. And Chloe was going to be very busy planning it.

When she thought of it like that, it seemed so straightforward. So simple. But instead, it all felt far too complicated.

"I'm in town all week," Lori surprised her by saying.

Even Nick looked shocked at this, and, dare Chloe think, not exactly pleased. "All week? What about work?"

"This is work, silly," Lori said, ruffling his hair.

He frowned and smoothed his hair.

Lori looked at Chloe and said, "My editor understands how important it is that this cover story is just right. She's given me the full week to devote to making sure everything will be perfect. So I'm all yours. We'll nail down the flowers, the invitations, the cake, everything. Oh. That reminds me. My editor and I were thinking that it would look really nice to have a sunset as a backdrop while we're saying our vows."

Chloe tried to process what she was hearing. Her eyes kept darting to Nick, who was now looking out into the distance, his jaw set.

"Well, your ceremony will be at five, which is a few hours before sunset. And actually, the sun sets in the west, so unless we went down to the part of the bay where it sort of slopes—"

"Oh, fine. We'll just Photoshop it if we have to," Lori said. "And another thing."

Chloe was almost afraid to hear it. "Yes?"

"The guests. We'll want the men in navy. The women in white, blue, or pink, preferably in the shade of...raspberry. It will be the most visually appealing."

Raspberry? Chloe stilled, wondering if Lori was actually being serious. It took a moment to realize that the precise shade of pink that Lori wanted her guests to wear was not the most shocking thing she had said.

"White?" Chloe hadn't heard this one before. "But usually the bride is the only one in white."

"But it's a beach wedding. And I don't need someone showing up in red and ruining the color scheme of the photos," Lori explained. "No, white. Pink. Blue. Even Navy. No yellow. No red. No black."

Chloe glanced up and down Lori's dress again but kept her thoughts to herself. "We'll make a note of the request in the invitation." She could only imagine what Jessica would say when she told her about that. They'd share a laugh, that much was sure. After all, in all her years owning Bayside Brides, Chloe had only ever heard of a bride trying to control a wedding party, not the entire guest list.

But then, more and more she wasn't so sure if this was a wedding or a photo shoot.

"Anyone who doesn't adhere can sit in the back, away from the photographers." Lori pointed a finger to the sky, as if just remembering. "Oh! And I almost forgot. The photographers will also need a bird's eye view for some of their shots. Can we secure a balcony at the hotel? And if the lighting isn't good, we'll need to bring in our own."

Nick muttered something under his breath that Chloe couldn't hear and that Lori didn't seem to catch.

"But we'll discuss this all in the morning. Eight work? Oh, it's so hot." Lori fanned herself and grimaced as she looked down at the lawn chair.

Chloe knew an opportunity when she saw one. "Let me grab you something cold to drink. I could use a refresh myself." It wasn't true, she thought, glancing down at her half-full glass of wine. Still, she took a sip. A long one. "Warm," she explained, pulling a face, and quickly moved aside, her heart pounding as she walked up the stairs to the deck.

She managed to smile at Margo and Abby, who were still seated near the grill, and she even said a quick hello to Kelly, who was counting out paper plates with Evie's help.

From across the lawn she heard the peal of laughter as Lucy and Bridget's daughter Emma chased a ball, and Bridget's warning from the near distance to be careful.

But it all felt hazy, like she wasn't really here at all. Her mind was a hundred miles away.

The kitchen was cool, and Hannah was alone, standing at the counter, cutting up vegetables and popping them onto skewers.

"Need any help?" Chloe offered. It would be the easiest excuse, she decided. Sure, onions made her eyes water, but right now, she already felt shaky, and on the verge of tears.

"If you're sure you don't mind?" But Hannah was already pulling another cutting board from a cabinet and sliding it to her.

Chloe set to work. Slowly. If she could, she'd stay in here all night. Offer to wash the dishes. Refill the drinks. Anything would be better than facing Nick and Lori right now. Tomorrow, when she was back at work, in a professional capacity, she would feel different.

Or so she hoped.

"So, I've been meaning to ask you about Lori," Chloe said as she peeled an onion. Her eyes were already starting to burn, but she didn't care. "Any personal anecdotes I should know to help me with their wedding planning?"

"Oh, we were never all that close," Hannah surprised her by saying.

"Oh. But since you invited her to the wedding…"

Hannah cut her a glance. "We were coworkers, really.

Went out for lunch. Two single girls. You know how it is. We lost touch until she reached out to me a few months ago because Nick was thinking about buying the hotel. She knew I was from here."

"Small world," Chloe commented.

"Not really," Hannah said. "Nick's mother is from here. Actually, the reason that Lori and I first got to be friendly at the magazine was because I mentioned I was from Oyster Bay and she said that this guy she knew had some family connections here too. That was before they were dating."

Chloe knew, of course, but she didn't elaborate.

"Anyway, when she reached out to me this spring, I hadn't heard from her in years. Not since we'd left the magazine. Then when she mentioned that Nick was coming to town, I mentioned Dan, and one thing led to another. It would have felt wrong to not invite her to the wedding," Hannah finished.

"Well," Chloe said, trying to wrap her head around all of this. "It seems to have all worked out that Dan can help Nick with the renovations."

"Maybe." Hannah widened her eyes. "I didn't know that they were planning to move to California after the wedding."

Chloe stopped chopping the onion. "California?"

Hannah skewered the last pepper from her pile. "Lori was out there over the weekend. The magazine we used to work for wants her back. Big position. Big opportunity.

She'd be crazy to turn it down. Of course, I don't think it's a done deal yet, though."

Chloe felt all the dots coming together, but still, she needed to hear it, just to be sure. "And what is she waiting on then?"

Nick, she supposed. To see if Nick would be willing to go to California. To give up his dreams for hers.

But Hannah said, "The wedding. They want to see how she handles the cover story. It's her first cover story, apparently, and the only reason I think she even got it was because it's her wedding and she promised her boss it would be made to suit their tastes. And, of course, Nick comes from a prominent family. They liked the idea of the heir to Tyler Hotels being on the cover."

Chloe clutched both glasses of wine in her hand. "You mean, this entire wedding and the cover story will determine if she gets the job at the fashion magazine?"

"It's a big position," Hannah said. "So it's a test of sorts. Not like that's any pressure for you," Hannah said laughing. "But as you can see, this wedding is very important to her."

"Yes," Chloe said. "But is it important for the right reason?"

She and Hannah exchanged a look, and Chloe knew they were both thinking the same thing.

"Don't tell her I said anything," Hannah said quickly. "I think she wants to keep this quiet, in case it doesn't work out."

"Has she told Nick?" Chloe blinked, trying to process

this information. Nick loved Oyster Bay. He wanted to stay. He wanted to grow that hotel. He wanted to put down roots. And he hoped that Lori would too.

"You don't think he'd have a problem with it, do you? I mean, he must travel all the time for work. His company buys hotels all over the country."

Chloe nodded. She supposed that part was true, but still, she couldn't help but feel that Nick deserved to know the truth, and sooner rather than later.

But she wasn't the one to be telling him.

"I'm going to say hello to Melanie," she said, clinging to the first person she saw walk through the sliding glass door, even though she saw Melanie every day. "Mind bringing this to Lori?"

Hannah took the glass with a smile. "Sure. I'll see you out there?"

"Sure," Chloe said, a little less enthusiastically. She walked over to Melanie, but not to say hello. She made a polite excuse about needing to talk to Jessica about the invitations, and then, making sure that no one else noticed, she slipped out the front door.

Chapter Twelve

Chloe met Lori before she went into work, at Angie's, mostly because she needed an extra dose of caffeine after a sleepless night. Lori hadn't implied that Nick would be joining, and Chloe couldn't hide her relief when she looked up from her second cup of coffee to see that Lori was alone.

She was impeccably dressed, as always, this morning in a white sheath dress with a colorful statement necklace that matched her gold strappy heels.

She didn't bother ordering a coffee, but just took a seat and pulled out a binder. A large binder.

"My," Chloe remarked when the binder thudded on the table. She had to slide her own papers to the side to make room, and she looked around the room to suggest another table, but of course, it was morning, it was summer, and well, this was Angie's. Every table was taken.

As her eyes did one final sweep of the room, they locked with a woman who was seated at a table, a thick planner in front of her. She was watching Chloe as if she knew her, and for a moment Chloe considered that she was a potential bride, until she spotted the band on her left hand.

She gave a tight smile and looked away. She pulled in a big breath, releasing it slowly. So Lori was finally ready to plan the wedding. And by the looks of it, she'd been busy.

"I know you sent me ideas for the flowers, but I've decided to go in a different direction," Lori said. She tapped a photo of an oversized bouquet of mixed flowers in shades of lavender, indigo, and white. It was stunning, but Chloe already saw one problem.

"I'm not sure if that would match the blush-colored bridesmaid dresses," she ventured, holding her breath.

But Lori just dismissed that with a casual wave. "Of course it wouldn't. That's why we're changing the color scheme."

"Changing the color scheme?" But Lori had already given her consent on the blush lining to the invitations. Not to mention the bridesmaid dresses that Chloe had assumed they would be finalizing today so she could place the order—for rush delivery. Now she'd have to pull up fabric swatches, and once Lori made her choice, go over the style options available.

A two-day set back, she thought, trying to calm herself. One, if Lori was decisive.

"Blush is too…too pink," Lori explained. "We need to evoke a real sense of mood for the cover. And since you made a good point about the sunset, it makes no sense to focus on sherbet colors. So let's stick with the blue family. My bridesmaids will be in lavender."

Chloe made a note of this. Lavender would be pretty. Elegant. Timeless.

"And the invitations?"

"They'll have to be changed, of course."

Chloe bit her lip. Last night after coming home from the party, she'd called Jessica to add the note about guest attire. There had been a long silence on the other end, and then, eventually, Jessica had muttered, "Are you serious?"

All too serious, Chloe realized. This was the wedding of her career. And from what she'd heard from Hannah last night, it was the wedding of Lori's career, too.

She eyed her client across the table, fighting the urge to ask if she had talked to Nick yet, if he knew. But this wasn't her secret to share anymore than it was to keep. She was just the wedding planner, she reminded herself. What went on between a couple really had nothing to do with her.

"I can see if Jessica can stop the order—"

"Well, I never committed to anything," Lori said, and Chloe stared at her. That technically wasn't true. "I never signed off on it," Lori continued. "That was just discussion."

Chloe had the sense that Lori was treating the vendors

of Oyster Bay as if they were on staff at *Here Comes the Bride* magazine. She took a deep breath.

"If an order has been placed, then Jessica has already paid for them," she said delicately. She knew that Jess was just starting out, and while growing fast, her invitations were freelance, her paper was purchased especially for each order, and the printing was a big portion of the cost. She didn't have a stock room or even a storefront to pull from. But she was good at what she did. And Chloe didn't want to take advantage over what was turning into a massive misunderstanding.

Lori didn't appear flustered. "I'm sure you'll find a way to make things right. That's your job, after all."

Yes, Chloe thought, swallowing hard. This was her job. Her dream job. The job she wanted, the business she loved. Difficult brides were a dime a dozen. But this…this was something different.

"Nick and I had a menu tasting," she started, hoping to turn the conversation to an item she could scratch off her list.

"He told me." Lori wrinkled her nose. "I'd prefer an outside caterer. The lunch I had there wasn't very good."

"Well, the chef only oversees the dinner service, and events, of course. Breakfast and lunch at the hotel are more casual." When Lori didn't bite, Chloe added, "Nick enjoyed the food we tried."

"Oh, Nick." Lori leaned into the table, as if she had a secret to share. "I swear that man would eat anything, and lately, he has! I'm getting nervous he won't even fit into his tux!"

Normally, this would have sent up alarm bells for Chloe, but right now, she couldn't help but feel defensive of Nick. She felt her heart tug when she recalled the way his stomach rumbled all through their tasting.

She sighed deeply and picked up her coffee. No sense feeling proprietary. Nick was an adult. He knew what he was doing.

And he knew who he was marrying.

But that part, she just wasn't so sure of anymore.

"He doesn't understand what this wedding means," Lori pressed, shaking her head.

Chloe knew she should refrain, say nothing, smile politely and say of course they would hire outside caterers. But she felt the need to defend Nick. And the hotel that he loved.

"And what does this wedding mean?"

Lori blinked. "Excuse me?"

Chloe had gone too far, and she recovered quickly, saying, "It helps me with setting a mood. The personal details."

Lori folded her hands on the table. "The only thing you have to worry about with this wedding is what will look good on camera. Would I have preferred pink bridesmaid dresses? Sure. But this isn't about what I want. And it's not about what Nick wants either. The wedding will still be beautiful. More importantly, it will be a success."

Not long ago, Chloe might have been guilty of this type of thinking herself, but perfection wasn't everything. In fact, it was starting to feel downright empty.

"I completely understand your concerns about the hotel," Chloe said, even if she didn't, and even if many other brides had been completely satisfied with their receptions held there. Even if Josh was not only a hardworking, good person, but also an excellent chef. "If you'd like, I can ask the chef to prepare a custom menu, just for your wedding. We can feature some of your favorite foods, as a personal nod to the bride and groom. The chef is a friend. I am sure he can accommodate your wishes."

Lori hesitated. "I suppose that would be more convenient. So long as he understands what's at stake here."

Oh, he did. And Chloe was starting to understand too.

"I'll call him after this. Or better yet, I'll stop by. I really think that since we're going with the country weddings theme, we should probably keep everything local to Oyster Bay."

Lori didn't look pleased, but she didn't disagree either.

"I suppose that will be cohesive, from a reader's point of view."

Chloe struggled not to widen her eyes as she turned back to her own task list. She forgot all about her coffee as they went through the other items that needed tending, many of which seemed to have been changed since their conversations last week.

Their conversations before Lori's trip to California, was more like it.

She was already exhausted by ten, when Lori finally left to make some calls to the office, and she stared into her coffee mug, frowning.

"Excuse me?"

Startled, Chloe looked up, surprised to see that it was the woman she had noticed earlier. "Yes?"

"I couldn't help but overhearing your conversation. You're the owner of Bayside Brides?"

Chloe's smile relaxed. "Yes. And you are?"

"Liz Cohen." The woman extended a hand. "I'm the owner of an event planning company opening later this month, just down the street."

Chloe felt the smile slip from her face. So here it was, then. The competition. She took the woman in. A few years older than her. Tweed pink skirt. Silk blouse. Nude stiletto pumps. Glossy hair cut in a bob.

She was all business. The entire package.

But Chloe was a better wedding planner, she reminded herself, thinking back to Saturday night.

Her heart began to race. Surely she hadn't been…noticed? She wasn't about to be called out on crashing a wedding, was she?

But then she remembered what Nick had told her. That if anyone asked, to say that she was his plus-one.

She felt her shoulders relax. He had a way of calming her anxiety. Even when he wasn't around.

"Welcome to Oyster Bay," Chloe said.

"We already have an office in Shelter Port," Liz continued.

Oh, did they now? Of course, this was all the type of information she could have already known if she'd gone ahead and researched the company. But she'd thought she'd seen everything she needed to know at the wedding on Saturday.

She did her best to keep her expression neutral and nodded.

"Expanding to Oyster Bay seemed like the natural thing to do," Liz said. She handed Chloe her card. The cardstock was thick. The letters were raised. Chloe had had new cards drawn up in the spring when they'd expanded their services, and now she was wondering how hers measured up.

"We don't have a wedding planner on staff, at least, not specifically. We do a little bit of everything," she added. "If you're interested, give me a call. As I said, we have another office in Shelter Port."

In other words, more business opportunities. More security even.

Chloe felt her defenses waver and she smiled at the woman. "Thank you."

"I liked the way you handled that difficult woman," Liz said with a grin, and Chloe had to stifle a laugh. "And I've seen your work."

Chloe blinked, feeling flattered. But then she realized,

of course Liz had checked up on Bayside Brides. She was a savvy business owner, and just like Chloe, she'd scoped out the competition.

Only unlike Chloe, she had a strategy for handling it.

When Liz pushed out the door a moment later, Chloe caught Leah's eye at the counter, who gave a conspiratorial wink back at her. Chloe sighed as she thought about the conversation she'd had with Leah, and her enthusiasm to bake cakes for future weddings. She slipped the card into her handbag and stood up. Even though it was just a small square of cardstock, somehow her bag felt heavier when she pulled it into her shoulder.

*

Chloe didn't go back to the storefront. She called Melanie instead, told her the truth, that she had the Addison-Tyler wedding to deal with, only she wasn't visiting vendors right now.

Instead she went to the duck pond, but not in her running shoes. This time she sat on a bench with a bag of stale bread and tossed bits into the water, watching as the ducks swam for each piece, some more determined than others, some left behind.

She tossed her bread to the stragglers, trying to urge them forward, trying to give them opportunity, but some of them couldn't be helped, and some of them were happy to stay back, to let others forge ahead, to grab the bigger pieces, to take what they needed.

"That's just like you," a voice behind her said, and she

looked up to see her father standing behind her, staring into the water, his face lined and creviced, his hands deep in his pockets. "Always fighting for the underdogs. Even when you were little, you always tried to make sure each duck had a fair shot."

"Dad." She blinked at him. It wasn't often they were alone anymore. And it was less often that they talked about the past, even the happy times, the ones she clung to, even now. "I didn't know you still came here."

"Every once in a while," he said. He jutted his chin at her. "I'm surprised you aren't at work. It isn't like you to take a day off."

"No," she said with a sigh. "It isn't."

He motioned to the bench and she inched to the side, handed him a piece of bread.

"You know that it's okay to take a break once in a while. There is such a thing as working too hard, you know."

"I know. It's just…" She darted her eyes to him. She couldn't finish that thought.

"I hate to break this to you, sweetheart, but sometimes in life, well, sometimes it's not about hard work. Sometimes it's about plain and simple opportunity." He tossed a couple of pieces of bread into the water, and they watched as the ducks swarmed them. "Sometimes there's a big opportunity, but you're not in the right place. Sometimes there are no opportunities." He held up his empty hands. "Now that little guy over there is one of the fastest swimmers in the pond. But see him, over there, waiting for bread from that little boy?"

The little boy had chucked his last piece a few minutes ago. Chloe nodded. She understood.

"You can't control the world, Chloe," her father said. "You just have to work hard, stay true to yourself, and believe that good things will happen. That doesn't always mean it will all work out. But that's life."

"How can you say that when you know that it doesn't always work out?" She stared at him, wondering how he could even say such a thing.

"Sure, it hasn't always been easy, but I have a wife. A daughter. A lot of people don't have half of what I have."

Chloe thought hard about this. She fell into that bucket, didn't she? No spouse. No child. No one to come home to at the end of a hard day.

No one to talk to when she felt scared or troubled. Or sometimes, even when she felt happy.

But that part…feeling happy…that wasn't something that happened often.

Until she'd met Nick.

"Your mom and I are happy. We've always been happy. That's not to say that we haven't had hard times, but we've always had each other."

Chloe smiled at her father, wondering if things might have been different if she'd known this years earlier.

But maybe she just couldn't see it then.

"Thanks, Dad," she said.

"Anytime, sweetheart," he said. He sighed and patted

his hands against his thighs. "Well, I'd better get home before your mother wonders where I've gone off to. But first, there's a spot just behind that tree that has some beautiful daisies…"

Chloe laughed. "You mean?"

He set a finger to his lips. "Now don't go telling my secret. Wouldn't want to let your mom down."

"She loves her daisies," Chloe said.

"She loves you," her dad said.

Chloe watched him walk away until he disappeared behind the tree. She'd go home for dinner soon. And this time, when she thought of home, she wasn't thinking of her empty, spotless apartment.

She stared at the pond for a while longer, watching the water ripple as the ducks waded through, thinking of her father's words over and over until her eyes prickled with tears.

She'd thought that starting her own company would bring her happiness and relief. She'd thought that expanding her business would be too risky. She'd thought that after seven years of owning Bayside Brides that she would finally be able to steady the racing of her heart, that she would finally feel secure. That she would finally trust herself.

She listened to her head. Always. But she'd never listened to her gut. And she'd never trusted her heart. Or put it first.

And her heart was telling her that Nick was making a

terrible mistake.

And her gut was telling her that even though she knew the stakes, and she knew how good it would be for Bayside Brides to be featured on the cover of *Here Comes the Bride* magazine, that she wasn't the wedding planner for the job.

She tossed the ducks a few more crumbs, until the last of her bread was used up and the sun had started to fade, and only then did she stand up and begin the walk back to her empty apartment.

She had a lot to show for herself, but in many ways, she had nothing at all.

She tossed the empty bread bag into the trash bin near the exit of the park and then, with certainty, she reached into her handbag and pulled out Liz's card. And she tossed that into the bin too.

Chapter Thirteen

It was two o'clock by the time Nick wrapped up his meeting with Dan. The budget was set, the schedule in place. All that was left was to finalize the deal for the hotel. Construction could start by mid-September once the necessary permits were restored. Nick was confident that Dan could oversee the work without interrupting the daily operations at the hotel.

He should feel happy, he knew. He should feel excited.

But instead of seeing each passing day as one closer to securing his dream, he saw it as one day closer to the wedding.

And this wasn't how it was supposed to be. Jitters. Nerves. Whatever people called it, this wasn't how he wanted to go into a marriage.

He needed to talk to Lori. It couldn't wait any longer.

Lori was waiting for him on the terrace, an iced tea in front of her. She didn't notice when he approached. She was hunched over her phone, her eyes fixed on the screen.

He pulled out a chair and ordered an iced tea. Lori looked up and flashed a smile.

"Just have to get this email sent off."

He nodded, not that she saw. Was it always like this with her? Perhaps it was, at least recently, he realized. Their life in New York was busy, too busy. They never had time to slow down and relax. They never sat back and took in their surroundings.

Or each other. At least, not anymore.

"I've been thinking," Nick said. He waited, wanting Lori's full attention, but she kept tapping at her phone. He bit back a sting of irritation, but it was soon replaced by something deeper. Sadness, he realized, and defeat, and the security he needed to say what he had to say next.

"I think that we should slow things down." There. It was out.

Now she looked up at him sharply. "Slow things down? What do you mean?"

"This wedding is less than three weeks away," he said. "Are you really ready for that?"

"Of course not!" she exclaimed. "I mean, there's still the cake to order and the centerpieces to decide on, and then I have to select the bridesmaid dresses. But it will all get done. We have Chloe, and I've never missed a deadline," she added, laughing knowingly.

He pulled in a breath. "See, but that's just it. This isn't a deadline, Lori. This is our wedding. And I can't help but think that we're getting married for all the wrong reasons."

She stared at him, her eyes wide, her skin pale, and a part of him wanted to take it back, or maybe…to go back. To a place and a time where she was just Lori, the pretty girl who was a fixture at every family get together, who used to watch fireworks with him at the Fourth of July, and jump off the rocks with him into the cool lake water on lazy Sunday afternoons. The girl who had come to his mother's funeral and said nothing as he stood beside his father, but instead took his hand and squeezed it, because she knew, because she knew his mother, and she knew his past, because she'd lived it.

But he couldn't go back. And he was afraid that he couldn't go forward either.

She wasn't that girl anymore. She'd grown up. But more than anything, they'd grown apart.

She reached out, took his hand in hers, gripped it really, only this time it wasn't like that dreary, rainy day when his world was collapsing and he needed someone, anyone, to take his pain away. Now she held onto him as if she was the one who was afraid.

"Now, hold on. You're just nervous. It's normal. The date got pushed up and sure, that's overwhelming, but that just means that we're one day closer to getting married and spending the rest of our lives together." She was staring at him, her eyes deep and searching, her mouth a thin line.

"And what does that look like to you, Lori?" he asked. In all this time, he'd never asked, and neither had she. Perhaps she'd assumed, like him, that their lives would continue as they always had. Work in the city. A country house for weekends. Fireworks on the Fourth of July. Or maybe, he was wrong. Maybe she wanted something very, very different. "What do you really want out of life?"

She paused. "Well, I want the same things as you, of course."

He shook his head. "See, that's just the thing. I'm not so sure about that. Because the thing is…the thing is that you haven't asked what I wanted."

"Nick." Lori frowned, pulling back. "That's not fair. I know you wanted to get married here at this hotel."

"And you still tried to find a way to have it somewhere else," he said.

She said nothing to that. He sighed heavily. This wasn't about a venue or even a wedding date. This was about so much more. Something bigger.

Something irresolvable.

"It's partially my fault," he said. "I knew how much this wedding meant to you and so I let you take over. But I don't just want a wedding. I want a future."

"Well, of course we have a future. But we have all the time in the world for that." Lori's expression changed to something stern. "Everyone is expecting this, Nick. You and me…people saw that coming since we were kids.

Invitations are going out this week. Our parents—"

He shook his head. "My mother only had one expectation for me and that was for me to be loved, to love. And to be happy."

"Well, I meant your father. My parents." Lori hesitated. "But you are happy, aren't you?"

Nick looked down at his hand, still intertwined with hers. It was a hand he memorized, a hand he had held many times over the years, only it wasn't a hand that reached for him very often anymore. And it wasn't one that made him feel connected. Or loved.

"I'm not so sure I have been happy," he finally said. He looked at her sadly. "And I'm not sure that I can make you happy."

She pulled back, blinking rapidly. "If this is about California—"

He frowned. "California? What do you mean?"

Her cheeks grew pink and she swallowed hard, struggling to look him in the eye. "I thought maybe Dan told you."

He freed his hand and leaned forward. "Told me what?" When she didn't say anything, he repeated, "Told me what, Lori? What is this about California?"

She sighed and looked down at her hands. "I didn't tell you because I was waiting for it to be official. But the old magazine wants me back. It's a senior position, Nick," she emphasized, as if this should be fair explanation. "It's a once in a lifetime opportunity."

"In California," he said flatly.

"There are plenty of development opportunities in California." She smiled. "Your father told me that he was thinking of asking you to head up the West Coast team!"

"My *father* knew about this?" Nick's voice was louder than he'd intended. He leaned back in his chair, his mind spinning as he tried to take this all in. How long had this been planned? How many people were scheming behind his back?

How many people were trying to decide how he would live his life, without consulting him?

"When were you planning on telling me all this?" he ground out.

Lori swallowed hard. Her cheeks were blotchy and she struggled to meet his eye. "I think...I think your father was going to make an announcement, at the wedding. Sort of...like a wedding gift."

"A wedding gift." He stared at her. He couldn't even believe this.

"We just want what's best for you," Lori explained. "I know you have a sentimental attachment to this little hotel, but it's just one project. And California...the West Coast...there's a whole new world of opportunities for us."

Us. It was the first time she'd referred to them this way in a long time, but it wasn't about him at all.

Nick didn't speak for several seconds. He couldn't. His mind was spinning, imagining conversations that had taken place behind his back, his father and Lori, deciding on what would be best for him.

What would be best for them.

"I need to ask you one question, and I need you to be completely honest with me," Nick said, leaning forward. "Does our wedding have anything to do with you getting this job in California?"

There was a long pause. Too long. Long enough that he didn't need to hear the answer.

"How long has this been in the works?" he asked.

She hesitated. Finally, on a sigh, she said, "I applied for the job at the beginning of the summer."

"And that's why you jumped at the chance for the cover spot," he said, piecing it all together. "Our wedding on the cover was your chance to guarantee you oversaw a cover story. I'm sure that looked really good on your resume."

"It's not as terrible as you make it sound," Lori said.

"Unbelievable," he said, pushing back his chair and standing.

"Where are you going?" Lori asked, staring at him in shock.

"I don't know, Lori. I don't know where I go from here. But I know that I'm not going to California, and I'm sorry that I can't be who you want me to be. You deserve to be happy. But I do too."

He walked down the stairs, hurt burning in his chest and blinding his vision, not stopping until his feet touched the sand. Seagulls swooped up ahead and called out over the crashing waves. He pushed forward, against the wind, until he reached the water's edge, and only then did he look back, at the great, grand hotel, at the girl he once knew and once loved, who had somehow slipped away.

But what he saw now wasn't the past. It wasn't the ghost of his mother, or the child he once was. It wasn't even Lori, young and spirited, as she used to be, and maybe still could be…but not with him.

It was his future. It was where he wanted to be.

*

The next morning, Chloe came to Bayside Brides early, just as she usually did. She'd had her coffee and her breakfast, and each dish was rinsed, washed, and put away. She'd made her bed with hospital corners. But she had skipped her run. Lack of sleep would have made it pointless, and she was starting to think that it was okay to change her routine once in a while.

That maybe, it was when you dared to break away from the tried and true that good things started to happen, not just bad things.

Melanie was the next to arrive, and Chloe knew from a glance at their appointment book that they didn't have anyone scheduled for another hour. Sarah could handle the walk-ins. Sarah could handle a lot of things.

Chloe had put together a good team at Bayside Brides. The best really. And that was why she felt comfortable saying what she needed to say.

"I've decided to remove myself from Lori's wedding," Chloe said. She watched Melanie carefully, waiting for the fall-out reaction, the shock, the confusion, the protests, but all she got was a narrowing of her cousin's eye and a strange purse of her lips.

"This is about Nick, isn't it?"

Chloe frowned, but it was forced, and despite all her efforts to join clubs back in high school, drama had never been her strength. She was too much of a realist, she supposed.

"Why would you say that?"

"Because I saw the way you looked that one morning you came into the shop, a few days after Hannah's wedding. And I saw how you were after Lori introduced us to her fiancé." Melanie tipped her head. "You fell for him."

Literally, Chloe thought. She didn't pride herself on being witty, and if she was able to find any humor in this situation, she would have had a good laugh at that.

Instead, she looked her cousin in the eye. Melanie was her closest friend, her oldest friend, and her business partner. She was more than a cousin. She was her better half. And they'd always been honest with each other.

She was the one person who really knew Chloe. Really understood why she was the way she was. Of course she had figured this out.

"It doesn't matter how I feel," she said. "He's engaged."

"Yes, but is he engaged to the right person?" Melanie looked at her plainly.

Chloe couldn't argue with that. Still. "It's not our decision to make."

"But Bayside Brides is everything to you," Melanie pointed out. "It's not like you to let your personal feelings interfere. Are you sure you really want to step aside?"

Chloe nodded firmly. She'd thought about this long and hard all last night, and she'd woken from a restless sleep knowing what she had to do.

"This business is important to us," she said. "I don't want my personal issues to interfere with things."

"You really like him," Melanie said. It was a statement. Not a fact. And one that Chloe couldn't argue with.

"I do," Chloe admitted, feeling that tug in her chest again.

Melanie nodded slowly. "But won't Lori be expecting you to see this through? The wedding is less than three weeks away now."

"I know, and I'm planning to put Sarah on the bulk of the interactions where Nick is present. I can still talk to Lori, place orders, and oversee things. From a distance."

Melanie raised her eyebrows. "It would work. And Sarah would be thrilled."

"Thrilled for what?" Sarah asked, poking her head around the door.

Melanie glanced at Chloe, as if to confirm that this was really what she wanted to do. Chloe nodded, even though her heart felt heavy. What she wanted and what she should do were two very different things.

"I was hoping you could handle some of the meetings going forward with Lori and Nick," she said.

Once again, the reaction she was expecting was not given. Sarah winced and said, "I don't think that's going to happen."

Chloe stared at her. Was this not Sarah Preston, the very woman who leapt at any chance she had to help plan a wedding and was all too happy to offer up one of her back issues of the dozens of wedding magazines she had subscribed to since she was a child?

"It's a chance to be involved in a wedding featured in one of your favorite magazines," she reminded her now. Honestly, what was going on here?

"It's not that," Sarah said, looking uncertainly from Chloe to Melanie. "I was just coming in to tell you that Lori just called. To tell us that she won't be needing our services."

Now Chloe's hands stilled. She felt Melanie's eyes on hers as the room fell silent. Her mouth went dry as she stared at Sarah.

They'd been fired. They'd lost the cover article.

And it was all her fault.

She'd crossed a professional line. And it had cost her more than a golden opportunity.

It might have cost her her business.

And it had also cost her her heart.

Chapter Fourteen

It was another Saturday at Bayside Brides, and for at least two of their clients, it was wedding day. Chloe thought back on the two brides who had come into the shop at different times over the past year for the dress fittings, and despite both having chosen a sunny August day to say their vows, they couldn't have been more different.

"I hope that Gina isn't regretting all the beads on that dress," Chloe said, thinking of how heavy the garment had been.

"No more than Victoria will regret her ten-foot train," Sarah said, and all the women laughed.

"I have a feeling that both women got everything they ever wanted," Melanie assured them all, and Chloe knew that she was probably right, and not just about the dress. Both Gina and Victoria were marrying the loves of their life, in gowns they had chosen just for the occasion. It would be the happiest day of their lives, even if something went wrong, because they were both marrying for true love. In Gina's case, she had waited three extra years for this date, because her fiancé was in the service and had been deployed, and Victoria was a cancer survivor. There was a time when she hadn't been sure this day would arrive.

Chloe pulled in a breath, thinking of another wedding that was just around the corner, and then busied herself with a stack of inventory papers that she needed to update in the computer. There was no reason to dwell on that, and if she'd learned anything in recent weeks, it was that she had to break free of the past a little more often and focus on the present.

"Mail's here," Sarah announced, spotting the postal carrier out the window. She opened the door, letting in a burst of warm, sunny air, and collected the stack. "Bill. Bill." She rolled her eyes as she continued leafing through the pile, her face finally lighting up. "Oh! The newest issue of—"

Her face blanched as she stopped herself, and Chloe knew.

"We should probably cancel the subscription," Melanie said hastily.

"What? No. We have a business to run and we're here to serve brides. Add it to the table, Sarah," Chloe said.

Reluctantly, and only after a meaningful glance in

Melanie's direction, Sarah exchanged last month's issue of *Here Comes the Bride* with the newest.

"September issue?" Chloe asked, just to show that she was okay with it.

Sarah nodded, then wrinkled her nose. "Disappointing cover this month. I think that magazine is going downhill."

Chloe knew that Sarah was just being kind, and she was grateful for it, but it also made her think of Lori, and her plans that didn't include the wedding magazine at all, and that even if it did go downhill, Lori wouldn't be going down with it. Lori would be living happily ever after in California, with Nick.

But would Nick be so happy?

She glanced up to see Melanie frowning at her.

"We're having a slow day," her cousin said. "And you haven't had a day off in forever."

"If this is about being fired by Lori, you don't need to worry. It was a blessing, really." Chloe could tell that neither Sarah nor Melanie were convinced, and her own heart sank a little when she glanced at the glossy new cover of the magazine on the coffee table.

"I just hate to think of someone else getting the business when you did the brunt of the work," Sarah said.

It was true, and it was something she should probably remedy in the future. She'd considered having clients sign a contract for her planning services, but she'd managed to offset the risk up until now by having the clients put down the deposits as they went along, so that Bayside

Brides wasn't on the hook for anything.

She'd been lucky that Jessica had managed to stop the invitations from going to print. They never had agreed on a cake, and no flowers had been ordered. The band hadn't been chosen.

It had been a close call. Too close. And one to learn from.

Lesson one: don't fall for the groom.

"I wonder if they went with the new event planning company," Sarah said now.

Chloe shrugged. "Maybe. Or maybe they decided to use someone from New York." After all, now that Lori needed this wedding in order to land the job in California, the stakes had been raised.

"Well," Chloe said, stacking the inventory papers into a neat pile. "I should file these before our next appointment."

She walked into the back room quickly, hoping that the emotion wasn't evident in her expression, but a moment later Melanie came through the door, her face edged in concern.

"There isn't another appointment today. And I meant it when I said you should take the opportunity to leave early." When Chloe didn't respond, Melanie said, "I'm worried about you."

Chloe closed the file cabinet. "Why? Because of Lori?"

Melanie's look was frank. "Because of Nick."

Chloe shook her head, but there was no denying the

pull in her chest. She leaned back against the file cabinet, unable to drum up the energy to go back into the storefront just now.

"He's making a big mistake," Chloe said.

"I know. We all know. Maybe even he knows," Melanie said with a shrug.

True, so true, but did he know about California yet? Or did Lori plan to spring that on him after the wedding?

Chloe wrestled with this for a minute, just as she did every time she thought of it, but she always came back to the same decision, and this time she couldn't use her professional relationship with the couple as the excuse. This time, she could only base things on her personal feelings.

Nick was a grown man. He and Lori had history. And whatever had brought them to today and whatever would carry them into tomorrow had nothing to do with her. Nick had made that very clear when he hadn't even contacted her since Lori had fired their services.

It didn't matter that she had spent over a week working hard on this wedding. It didn't matter that Bayside would now lose national exposure in the magazine.

She didn't matter to Nick. Clearly.

And eventually, he would stop mattering to her too.

"You know, I think it's a good thing that you fell for Nick," Melanie surprised her by saying.

Chloe narrowed her eyes in suspicion. "Sorry, I don't see how falling for a man who turns out to be not only engaged but a client benefits me or our business in the slightest."

"He opened your eyes," Melanie said. "You didn't see it, but you were stuck in a rut. Work, work, work. All work and no fun."

Chloe resisted the urge to roll her eyes. It wasn't the first time she was hearing this. But hearing it again, she realized that she wanted it to be the last. She didn't like that description of herself. She much preferred the person she'd been the past few weeks. Around Nick.

"It's good to let people in," Melanie said, her tone a little more gentle. She and Chloe exchanged a look. They didn't need to say anything; Melanie just understood.

And maybe, if she let others know her the way Melanie did, they would understand too. That wouldn't be half bad, she considered.

"Well, Nick wasn't the one for me," she said firmly, reminding herself that their connection meant nothing in the end.

"Maybe not," Melanie said. "But now you know that if you're willing to put yourself out there, make room in your life for someone, that it feels good."

"It felt reckless, that's how it felt," Chloe said tightly.

"Well, that's because of the circumstances," Melanie pointed out. "But if you just think of Nick…"

Nick. She didn't want to think of Nick. But she did.

"It was exciting," she admitted. "And it was nice to think of there being more to my day than just Bayside

Brides."

Melanie gave a knowing grin. Chloe could tell she was resisting the urge to say, "Told you so."

"Don't lose hope just yet," Melanie said. "After all, you did catch Hannah's bouquet."

Now Chloe really did roll her eyes. "You know, I think I will take you up on your offer and head out a bit early."

Melanie looked nearly as surprised by the declaration as Chloe felt. As soon as the words were out, she wanted to take them back. What would she do? Go to the gym? Work was her refuge. It kept her focused and calm and kept those nagging insecurities from bubbling to the surface.

She glanced at the clock on the wall. It was only three. She had the better half of the afternoon stretched out before her, and the sun was shining through the windows. She could go to the beach. It was a reckless thought, and it thrilled her. Could she do it? Without fretting and worrying the whole time that the entire business would fall apart in her absence?

She looked at her cousin. Thought of Sarah. She trusted her team. And she trusted herself.

And she had to trust her gut too. And her gut told her that this parting of ways with Lori and Nick was all for the best in the long run.

"Here's your bag," Melanie said, taking it off the hook beside the door and thrusting it at her. "And you can take the back exit."

"My, you're in a rush to get rid of me!" Chloe almost

laughed, but her eyes were frantically scanning the room, wondering if there was anything that she was forgetting.

"I'm eager to get you out before you change your mind," Melanie said, raising her eyebrows.

Chloe grinned at her. "You know me too well."

"I do," Melanie said, and Chloe was grateful for it.

She may not have made much time for anything but work for a long time, but somehow, the people who mattered most had stuck by her. Her friends. Her cousin.

Her parents.

She waited until she had stepped outside, fairly certain that Melanie had gone so far as to lock the door behind her, and pulled out her phone. She had the day to herself. But she didn't need to spend it alone at all.

*

Two hours later, Chloe stood in her empty apartment, which she'd just spent the last twenty minutes cleaning, after spending a glorious afternoon browsing shops on Main Street and even treating herself to an ice cream. It wasn't on her regimen, but she figured that she would make up for it with her evening run. After all, she couldn't completely be expected to change overnight. And she didn't want to either.

All her life she'd feared change. Assumed only bad things came with it. Now she wanted to think differently. Believe that someday, without warning, someone would come along and shake things up a bit, just like Nick had done.

The bouquet that she had caught at Hannah's wedding was still in a vase on the coffee table, but it had become wilted and the petals were brown at the edges. She picked it up and carried it to the sink. She'd prolonged throwing it away, which wasn't like her. She knew it was silly, a tradition, that was all. And she hadn't even caught it, just grabbed it, by default.

She wouldn't be the next person from Hannah's wedding to get married, but thinking about it now, that night, Nick, and the whirlwind of the last few weeks, she knew that if the opportunity came along again, she'd be ready to take the risk. After all, she was in the business of love, wasn't she? She may as well hold out a little hope for herself.

With one last look at the flowers, she put them into the trash and then left the apartment. It wasn't her usual time for a run, but she had other plans for the evening. She was living on the edge, only this time it didn't feel reckless or exciting, it felt challenging. And she'd never been one to turn away from a challenge.

The duck pond wasn't far from her apartment, but she didn't want to go for a run there today, and not because she was worried about running into Nick. She had a feeling that these days Nick was keeping his workouts to the gym at the hotel, or maybe he was even back in Manhattan.

She decided to go to the beach, something she didn't do often enough, even though she lived so close to the shoreline.

The sun was still hot by the time she arrived, but the breeze blowing in off the ocean made up for the lack of shady trees that the park provided. Her ankle had healed, but she wasn't pushing herself quite as hard as she had done in recent weeks, and while this might have made her twitch just a month ago, today she felt proud of herself for getting back out there, first with the running, and later, eventually, with her heart.

She took the path down by The Lantern, thinking that it had been a long time since she'd frequented the restaurant owned by Hannah and Evie's father, and decided to make a point to stop in one night next week. Maybe Kelly would want to join her. Or maybe she'd make some time for the knitting classes that Kelly offered, see what all the fuss was about.

With the wind on her face, she began to jog, slow and steady, the sand moving under her trainers, the sound of the waves making it difficult to hear, but she strained for a voice, someone calling out.

"On your left!" the voice called, and she edged to the right, as far as she could, without getting her shoes wet.

"On your left!" the voice called again, and it was louder this time. Deep. Maybe even a little…amused?

Her heart picked up speed, but she didn't dare turn around. She didn't want to risk losing her footing again.

Besides, it wouldn't be him. Not like this, not here. Surely, if he saw her, he would turn, run the other direction?

The voice stopped, and Chloe frowned, wondering if that was exactly what had happened. If Nick had realized it was her, turned, and run the other way.

But then, just when she had given up, a man came up beside her, but he didn't run past. He altered his pace, in step with hers, and even when she stopped abruptly, he did too. Damn it.

"Nick." She was out of breath, but not from the running—being a stickler about her routine meant she was in better shape than that. But her heart was racing and she was caught off guard and she didn't know what he was doing here or what he wanted to say and oh, he looked good. Too good. His hair was blowing in the wind and there was something more relaxed about him than there had been all those other times. He looked at home here. At peace.

"Hello, Chloe." He gave her a slow, crooked smile that made her heart twist and her defenses flare up.

"Nick." She nodded, once. Put her hands on her hips. Willed her heart rate to return to normal.

"I was hoping to run into you. I've…been meaning to talk to you."

She held up a hand. "It's fine. Lori called the shop and let us know."

He frowned at that, looking at her closely. "I wasn't involved in that call, so I can't be sure what she said."

"Just that she didn't need my services after all." Chloe caught the pinch between his brows and ignored it.

Maybe her tone was too sharp. Or too bitter. Really, could she blame Lori?

"I'm sorry about this," Nick said, and he looked so sincere that she almost believed.

Maybe, she did believe him.

"I know that your business is important to you. I know that this article, this *cover story*, well, it would have been some nice press."

She raised her eyebrows. "Work isn't everything to me." Once it had been. Not anymore.

"And I'm sorry that the wedding has been called off," he said.

"Well—" She frowned. What had he just said? She looked at him sharply. His expression was blank, maybe even a little sad. "Wait. What did you say?"

"The wedding has been called off," he said again.

Now Chloe's heart was really hammering. She hadn't just lost the business. She'd done something much worse. She'd interfered, even when she'd tried not to. She'd fallen for the groom. And maybe…She searched his face. Maybe he had fallen for her too.

"What do you mean it's been called off? You and Lori…you have history."

"We have a past," Nick said, nodding. He looked at her squarely. "But we don't have a future. Chloe…"

She shook her head, backing up a bit. "You don't want to have regrets, Nick."

"The only regret I have is that I let it go on as long as

it did," Nick said.

"Wedding jitters are normal," Chloe stressed. She locked his gaze, begging him, to go back to Lori, to make this right, even when she knew Lori was all wrong for him.

"These weren't jitters," he said. "They were…feelings."

She blinked, unable to reply to that, not sure what he meant.

"I've wanted to talk to you, Chloe. I wanted to explain. But I just needed time on my own to clear my head. Business helped with that," he said, giving her a quirk of a smile.

She felt her shoulders relax. "I understand that."

"You understand a lot of things. Lori didn't, not in the end." He took a step toward her, but she stiffened.

"You can't compare us. Please don't put me in this position."

"I'm not comparing you. And my feelings for you have nothing to do with Lori."

Feelings for her. He'd actually said it. That connection hadn't been imagined.

She should feel happy. Elated. But she had never felt more miserable.

"I was going to step away from the wedding anyway. You don't know me—"

"But I want to know you better," he said, stepping forward.

She stepped back, managing to get her shoe wet, and

she didn't even care.

"You're not the reason that I ended things with Lori. Well, not fully." Nick said, and Chloe didn't know whether to feel relieved or horrified.

She didn't want any part in it. That was why she hadn't told him about California. About Lori's plan.

She looked at him squarely. Of course. He had found out all on his own. The way he needed to.

"Lori and I wanted different things. From life. And from this wedding."

Chloe nodded. She couldn't argue with that. "And you really didn't think you could be happy?"

"I'm happy here, in Oyster Bay. I'd made it a goal, a long time ago, to return to this town. My mother brought me here for a reason, and…I think this is where I was meant to be."

"And Lori?"

"Lori's chasing her dream," Nick replied. "And I'm chasing mine."

"And what does that look like?" Chloe asked, holding her breath.

He smiled. "Well, it starts with…dinner? If you're free. And willing."

Dinner. She could do that. She wanted to do that. But not tonight. "I'm heading over to my parents' house for dinner," she said. "But…tomorrow I'm free."

He gave her a slow grin. "Perfect."

"I thought you didn't like that word." She swatted his

arm, and he used the opportunity to pull her in, wrap his arms around her waist. He felt warm, solid, and right. So right. He leaned down, kissed her softly on the lips, once, twice, just enough to leave her heart fluttering.

"Better than perfect," she said. Because it was.

Made in the USA
Monee, IL
16 November 2020

47987869R00135